CONVERGENCE

THE DANDELION TRILOGY
BOOK 3

ALSO BY MIKE FRENCH

The Dandelion Trilogy
Book 1 – The Ascent of Isaac Steward
Book 2 – Blue Friday

CONVERGENCE

THE DANDELION TRILOGY
BOOK 3

MIKE FRENCH

Elsewhen Press

Convergence
First published in Great Britain by Elsewhen Press, 2013
An imprint of Alnpete Limited

Elsewhen Press, PO Box 757, Dartford, Kent DA2 7TQ
www.elsewhen.co.uk

British Library Cataloguing in Publication Data.
A catalogue record for this book is available from the British Library.

ISBN 978-1-908168-26-9 Print edition
ISBN 978-1-908168-36-8 eBook edition

Printed and bound by CPI Group (UK) Ltd, Croydon, CR0 4YY

FOR
PHILIP AND JENNY
AS TRUE AS I LOVE YOU

CONTENTS

WELCOME 15

THE WORLD OF UNDERSTANDING 19

THE WORLD OF IMAGINATION................. 167

She sees in movement,
the sense of a promise.
Motion slowing,
towards perpetual paths.

I chose you before all that would unfold,
before I became what I am now.
My dreams have deserted me,
filled my mind with a barren wasteland.
The smell of you the memory of winter,
the shape of you the sum of all my desires.
Together we will find the land of our hearts,
everything will become all that we can ever be.

Welcome

PROLOGUE

The bark is a skin weathered by sun, wind, rain, snow. A history of time marked out as the tree orbits the sun. Rings growing ever outward around its pith like the planetary halo of a large planet. Its heartwood stronger than iron, rising water in its sapwood bringing life from soil to stars.

Durram

She'd talk to Pete tonight – ask him the question. Turning, she walked back to the man she had killed, the smell of blood like rust, the smell of the inanimate. When would these people learn, she thought, the family was sacred, pure, a thing of beauty in a world of commerce and greed.

A canopy of mottled greens encircle the tree, a wood without end: the white froth of clouds dancing upon them. Rivers below flowing like liquid gold in the dappled sunlight. Questions thrown as seeds into the wind looking for soil to take root, to explain, to answer: why?

Pete

Pete's heart, hard like granite within his flesh and blood, increased in tempo. The digital overlay of the landing pad below, expanded and contracted like the motion of a jellyfish ascending to shallow waters. Thermal sensors picked up the outlines of two adults and a child.

In the air around the tree are the sounds of stories diffused into heart beats, rhythms left over from words. The folly of man looking for understanding held by roots in ancient earth. What endures is woven into the landscape: beauty, love, hope, connection.

Covenant

Leviticus looked at Covenant; her bronze body radiant, glowing as if pregnant. Her breasts firm, lips moist. She reached out and placed Leviticus' hand on her breast.
"Would you mind if I called you Isaac, here?"
"What?"
"And you could call me Rebekah if you wanted to."

Darkness throws the scene into stark contrast. The sky angry, brooding: waiting for change. The wood bright, resilient: trees edged with glowing light. A small bird flies over the topography passing bluebells, grasses, broad evergreen leaves.

Within the tree are the man and the woman. The colours and light of the wood pass over them like sheets of billowing russet. Skin, bone, bark and fern become one. They watch a great waterfall, their eyelids flickering to slow their perception of time – water droplets become gems of blue jasper suspended in the air.

They climb, finding connection with their fingers in the wooden skin, until they sit looking out over the wood, their hair blowing in the wind, their bodies tinged in blue. They scatter colours from the sky as the sunlight hits their skin, as if their beads of sweat are dustings of sapphires and amethyst.

Gabriel

The devastation reflected over the curvature of his blue eyes. The fire, which had burned deep within him, rose with sulphur flames to the surface. As the rage approached his black pupils, they dilated to allow the flames an easy passage.

Man, fire, machines, hate, violence; all pound at the door wanting to be let in. Doctrinal keys fail in locks responding only to the voices of those woven into narratives: the story is everything. And everything will become the story.

THE WORLD OF UNDERSTANDING

CHAPTER 1

Pete laid out the Generation Game trading cards that he had stolen from Durram's flat after her death. He began arranging them alphabetically starting with Anthea Redfern, then Bruce Forsyth, Graham Norton, Isla St Clair, Jim Davidson, Larry Grayson, Rosemarie Ford and Roy Castle.

The next day, he returned to find a burglar climbing out of the back window with his treasured trading cards. He took his Smith & Wesson and shot the thief five times in the back.

After dumping the body in the Adriatic, he walked to the Nautika restaurant. On the way, he passed a pretty young woman with freckles and a limp, who smiled at him. He stopped, introduced himself and by lunchtime was lying beside her on the grass with a bottle of Dom Pérignon and a punnet of strawberries. After a few days, when she asked about the trading cards he kept by the bed, he grew upset and threw her out: she limped down the moonlit street in tears.

That night, frustrated, Pete rang for a prostitute. Twenty minutes later there was a knock at his door and a redhead stood before him smiling. He welcomed her in, took her coat, looked at her suspenders and the ladybird pattern on her Playtex push-up bra and instructed her not to touch his trading cards.

When she asked him in a Polish accent if he would like to take a bath with her first, he instructed her no, could she read him a Julian Barnes book. When she asked him why, he replied that he liked a book at bedtime and please could she not ask any more questions. Raising an eyebrow she carried out his instructions and sat at the end of the bed. Half-way through, Pete fell asleep and she shrugged and carried on reading.

In the morning when she overcooked his poached egg, he grew angry, produced his gun and forced her to hand over all the takings from her earlier clients. She called him a fuck-head and left, slamming the door.

At this point Pete wondered if things were going well.

To calm himself he took a walk around the old city walls and smoked his favourite brand of cigarette.

Things sped up at that point.

He shot a dachshund that strained at its leash towards him, made love to the brunette who sat under the statue of the poet Ivan Gundulić in Gundulić Square, saved a small child on holiday from drowning, prevented an armed robbery at Dubrovnik Treasures and just before lunch ran onto the football pitch at Gradski stadion Lapad, after knocking off a *policajac's* cap, and scored the winning goal for NK GOŠK Dubrovnik.

In the afternoon, he rested for a while in the bath. Afterwards, he dressed as Napoleon to watch the Generation Game on television.

It was all rather unsatisfying. He had become acutely aware that he was rather shallow, only liked pretty women and had a tendency to lose his temper. An insight that was proved correct when the phone rang. It was the newspapers wanting to interview him about scoring the winning goal. He told them he was watching Bruce Forsyth and to go fuck themselves. Then he ripped the phone out of the wall and beat himself with it.

The day ended with him covered in blood, lying on the carpet with one arm tucked in his waistcoat. Two prostitutes sat on the sofa cutting cocaine using the edge of his trading cards whilst watching Bewitched.

In the morning he freshened up, then listened to the explanation of the damage to his cards from the two girls who were sitting eating toast. After he had tied them up in the basement he left for the airport and bought a ticket from Dubrovnik to London.

During the flight he listened to the story from one of the stewardesses about her jealous husband whom she had killed a year ago and who now flew with her on each trip, hidden in the cargo bay below their feet. He had, she explained, wanted to be closer to her to make sure she wasn't flirting, this was her way of accommodating that request. Pete, bemused, nevertheless enjoyed revealing her 36-D Fantasie moulded bra in the toilet; and when he disembarked she kissed him on the side of the cheek and handed him a bottle of champagne.

In the airport lounge he searched for Durram and spotted her standing holding a cardboard sign of his name in one hand and a black umbrella opened in the other. She kicked her foot back in the air as they embraced.

Ladies and gentleman, the game has started, let me introduce you to Peter Furst, possibly the greatest guy that has ever lived.

That had been a damned lie.

Pete disconnected from the game. That is, he thought, the last time I will ever play that. It was called SANTA – a total immersion game that worked by analysing embryonic subconscious decisions to form a Fractal map. Game play choices were then made according to this blueprint.

Pete felt violated. He believed himself to be a man of God and above such base desires. Yet apparently he was angry, shallow, impatient and, like most people, focused primarily on his own needs. He was fixated on one woman but his head would turn in an instant at a short skirt and a great pair of tits.

In many ways he was the everyman. He had both the desire to be with every pretty woman and the desire for there just to be the one. For Pete the one was Durram. The rest were roughly numbered in their billions.

CHAPTER 2

USA: Virginia: The City of Alexandria

Durram Brittle had the same dream every night.

A shadow would fall over the land. At first it appeared as if it were a great white shark, but then it shifted to become the outline of a passenger plane cutting across the solar stream. Pulsating as the land rose and fell, it moved towards her before snatching her up into the air.

She was in the plane. The engines had failed. The 'fasten seat belt' light had come on. Voices, instructions, shouting, someone praying. Durram wondered if she could remember how to get into the brace position. Should she make sure the children had fastened themselves in or connect her own belt?

She should fasten her belt.

She was about to die.

She was too young to die.

She couldn't see the kids. The fear of death rose over her, dark, brooding, hungry: she couldn't breathe. The animal instinct for survival battled with her natural desire to protect her children, the two forces clashing like titanic monsters within her skin and bone.

Before her a panoramic view of a wood opened up.

The rows before her started disappearing.

Where was the front of the plane?

People were dying.

What the hell was going on?

She must save herself at all costs.

Then she saw her children running towards her, their arms open.

And that would be it. She'd wake before the children reached her. Return to her bed.

This morning Durram lay for what seemed hours after waking: her limbs distorted like a collapsed marionette. One arm stuck out from under the covers. She couldn't find the will to get up. It was as if her blood had become liquid wax which had hardened in the cold of the night to petrify her.

She had wanted to go to bed early, after all today was a big day and it may have been her last night on Earth. But the lure of The Generation Game had proved too strong and she had sat watching it into the early hours of the morning reinforcing her memory of the prizes on the conveyor belt. She was now pretty sure that she could remember every item from every show and the order in which they had appeared.

A bumble bee hovered over the carpet, sending out a high-pitched wake-up call. It remained there for a moment as if it were a tiny helicopter awaiting instructions. Durram thought of Pete and wished things had worked out differently. She could never see him again. Never. Her regret at this was softened only by the knowledge it wouldn't have worked, not unless there had been some fundamental shifts in his attitudes and behaviour.

Durram realised that she was crying and rubbed her eyes with her hands to draw away the sorrow.

The bumble bee rose up towards the light of the window and settled on the glass. Durram remembered sitting in the garden the day before, wanting everything, for once in her life, to come good. She had photographed a dandelion pushing up under the shade of the red maple tree. The light of the late afternoon had caught it and thrown it into contrast. By focusing on the background she had created the illusion of a glowing ball of light hovering above the soil like a small sun.

The memory brought action. Durram swung her legs over the edge of the bed, put on her glasses and picked up her packet of cigarettes. She ran her finger along the inscription on the back of her silver lighter, it read, *To my Mary Poppins love Pete X.* Within her heart a Victorian roundabout span pumping blood out to her arteries. Its painted horses in a perpetual dance like the Israelites going around and around in the wilderness seeking redemption. She lit a cigarette, put it to her lips and waited a moment before slowly grinding it into her arm. The Israelites had spent forty years in the desert until all their fighting men had died. Durram didn't think she'd last that long, her journey was almost complete.

Under the shower she tried to find the strength in her to grasp hold of something outside of herself, but she just stood staring off into some distant point without end. When the shower spluttered and failed, she showed no emotion but quietly and calmly opened the door. After drying herself she pulled on some knickers and a T-shirt. Downstairs, she drank a glass of cold water from the tap and, opening the patio doors, stepped out into the morning.

The air smelt sweet and the freshness of dawn woke her as she walked over to the red maple tree. In her mind she visualised holding the dandelion up to her lips. She would blow gently. Make a wish as the seeds took to the air.

When she got there she felt a mixture of sadness and excitement. The seeds had flown in the night and she wasn't sure if that meant she had lost her chance or if something greater than her had already set them in motion.

Feeling incredibly foolish and full of wonder at the same time, she returned to the house to eat breakfast and to strip and clean her rifle.

CHAPTER 3

USA: Washington: The White House

Light streamed up in a vertical beam at the end of Reagan's bed. His eyes opened wide. Everything Must Go, by the Manic Street Preachers, played inside his head. Bathsheba played with his hair.

The scanner started moving its way along the mattress. Bathsheba pushed herself up onto her hands and smiled. Reagan started to panic – the scan would show he wasn't married to her; he hadn't long. He watched as the beam passed under them, sending shafts of light around the curves of Bathsheba's sports bra and onto the ceiling.

He could hear footsteps in the hallway.

Shouting.

He was in the White House. They'd protect him here – wouldn't they?

"Are you okay, Mr President?" said Bathsheba. "You've gone white."

The door shattered. Splinters of wood entered the room at high speed, piercing Bathsheba's flesh. She screamed, felt her side, looked at the blood on her fingers.

The Family Protection Agents burst in. Reagan saw them as a blur until they paused mid-flight suspended in the air. He read the ID badge of the agent closest to him. It read:

> Lieutenant Uriah
> Family Protection Agency

The room went red. The sound of an alarm jolted the action in the room back into fluidity. Uriah pushed Bathsheba off the bed, rolled Reagan onto his side and handcuffed him.

"You have the right to remain silent."

"Please don't tell Nancy," screamed Reagan.

Reagan opened his eyes; he had nodded off. The end credits to Goodbye, Mr. Chips were rolling on the wall. Bubbles span and bounced upward past his twelve toes.

"I hope you enjoyed your little nap," said his Chief of Staff, handing him a drink.

"I want Uriah killed."

"Of course, Mr President. He was killed a week ago in Afghanistan as you requested."

"Really?" said Reagan, turning to face his Chief of Staff. Orange blossom slipped up the side of the glass.

"Insurgent arranged it all."

Reagan turned off the foot spa and took a towel from his Chief of Staff. "Good – killed on the front line. Well then the way is clear. I can marry Bathsheba now."

"Very good, Mr President. Congratulations."

"Thank you. I think I'll get married in my boots and jeans back at the ranch."

"A splendid idea, Mr President."

"She is beautiful." Reagan sighed, his gaze became obscured by clouds of desire. "I first saw her bathing in the rooftop pool at the Ubud Hanging Gardens – amazing place: all green and lush. She was floating there as if suspended above the forest. I couldn't take my eyes off her."

"As you have said a number of times, Mr President."

"You don't think I'm too old for her?"

"Of course not, Mr President."

"You're a terrible liar, John."

"Thank you, Mr President, I learnt from the best. It's time for your jelly beans, sir."

"It is? Good, of course." Reagan stood, wobbled then brushed his hands down his suit and straightened his tie.

A small red dot appeared on his forehead.

"I want at least ten jokes about the Russians in my speech to Congress."

"There are no Russians, Mr President, they left Earth years ago."

"Just write the jokes, John."

"Our common enemy," began The Chief of Staff, as Reagan bent down to pick up his slippers, "are the Belgians–"

ZING.

THUMP.

"I love a good commie joke," said Reagan. He laughed and looked at the paisley wallpaper as if it were a mighty crowd swirling before him. "How is the Star Wars project coming on, John – I heard Disney was getting involved? John? John, why are you lying on the floor? Get up man."

A pool of blood seeped through the wool twist, the sound of footsteps, Reagan turned. A small bullet hole in the top right hand corner of the White House's window let in the cold autumn air.

It started snowing.

Reagan's wrinkled hand moved out before him and intercepted the laser marker. He recalled sitting as a boy on the front row of class straining to read the chalk markings. A wet stain appeared on Reagan's trousers. He swallowed, laughed, saluted, thought, "Oh no, not again."

CHAPTER 4

People passed by, as if following tramlines in the concrete: the blaze of moonlight above them powering their daily routines. At some point the sun had disappeared, vanished without trace as if it had only ever been parked for a while whilst God nipped into the local shop to buy some fags.

Everything should have stopped. The end of the world. Frozen planet. Certain death. There had been panic as clouds started to fall from the sky as orange snow and the surface of the seas started to freeze, but things became pretty much the same once the moon lit up – although the axis of the Earth did tend to wobble as it travelled through space released from its solar embrace.

Nobody knew why or how a body as small as the moon could become a bright orb in the sky – the probe to investigate had never returned and no one could account for the fact that the moon radiated just the right amount of heat and light to sustain life. But then, on the whole, people were more interested in watching the Generation Game.

Chief amongst them was Durram. Although that was last night, before the bumble bee, the dandelion and the recurring plane crash. Now, instead of watching Bruce Forsyth, her finger was curled around the trigger of her sniper rifle. After her breakfast that morning of pancakes drizzled in maple syrup, she had made her way along George Washington Memorial Parkway past Ronald Reagan Washington National Airport and crossed the Potomac River. She could see Reagan in the cross hairs. She hadn't enjoyed killing Uriah: she had lost the thrill of the hunt over the last year and now as she watched the clone of Reagan she felt bored, as if she couldn't really be bothered despite the years of preparation. But she needed to take attention away from her primary target, The Chief of Staff who now lay dead. And so like or not it was time to kill the puppet, for that truly was all that Reagan was.

Durram's subconscious adjusted her Méliès retinal implants to sharpen the image and splice layers of data into the scene. Her glasses only a vanity, the implants more than capable of correcting for her myopia, hung folded at the neckline of her T-shirt.

Durram pictured the bullet piercing brown twisted yarn, organic cotton, skin, flesh, cardiac muscle. The Avodah drug used to increase her work ethic within her altering her time perception, her brain reconstructing reality with everything slowed down. It gave her time to think.

It started to snow.

Reagan turned in slow motion and looked out of the window.

In the same amount of time Durram calculated two hundred and fifty three different outcomes to the shot, traced the trajectory of each path, worked the percentages of death depending on which organs she hit.

Reagan saluted.

The grass on the White House lawn peeled back as if it were skin to an orange. Machinery surged out of the ground. Red lights flickered along the edge of tubes, and where before there had only been moonlight between Durram's bullet and Reagan's heart, there now stood tower upon tower of military grade hardware. A hum filled the air.

Durram activated her digital attack software implanted in her head. The spatial distortion software time jumped a few seconds in the future so she could see where the shot would strike. She smiled, seemed to change her mind and moved the cross hair over to the air to air missile launcher pointing at her.

Perfect.

Durram pulled the trigger.

The bullet glanced off the missile launcher, pierced the side of the window, ricocheted off the desk and entered Reagan's body just under his left arm.

At the same time Durram felt something enter the back of her shoulder. She turned and looked through the haze of white. There were two CIA agents on the roof. A third was running towards her: snowflakes spinning in slow motion about his boots. Durram could sense the flow of air around him and calculated the time to traverse the distance, adjusting her data for the acoustic dampening of the fallen snow. He was moving at thirty nine miles per hour: operating at near one hundred percent of his enhanced contractile speed. Durram knew him well: he had a family, two kids called James and John, a dog, two cats, a snake and an iguana called Blake.

Durram succumbed to the blackness as her vision tunnelled in response to the adrenalin. Avodah in her bloodstream pulled at her as she slipped out of consciousness. She had been conditioned to withstand it – its use a necessary evil to help her stay under cover and to increase her performance within the work-addicted CIA. Her acceptance as a sniper to help protect the White House had taken years, but the Americans were pushing to outlaw the Protection of Family Act. They had to be stopped. The Chief of Staff had even sold arms to the Overtime Underground Network.

Durram knew she would die.

The world of Avodah beckoned, offered a delay, a paradise.

All had come to pass.

And so it was.

She wondered, as she reached down to her knife in her boot, what her clone had felt when Trent shot her.

The circus tent appeared at the edge of her vision. She could hear the ringmaster calling her, the sound of leaves rustling, birdsong.

"Our Father, who art in heaven," Durram gripped the knife, the blade towards her. "Hallowed be thy Name."

Footsteps behind her, helicopters over the White House. The sound of clowns, laughing, clapping from within the canvas of the big top.

"Thy kingdom come."

Her strength faded. She floated down inside the tent and looked at the ringmaster, "Welcome, Durram, to the wonderful world of Avodah."

"Thy will be done–"

Durram plunged the knife into her chest.

CHAPTER 5

ENGLAND: London: Vadim Tower

Eve poured herself a cup of freshly brewed coffee and looked out over the London skyline. A white fishnet cropped top wrapped around her vinyl bra. By her side a vase of cut flowers formed an oasis of pastel colours in the neon world she inhabited.

When she had first started she thought she could handle the sex, these days she wasn't so sure. The cause was true but she had lost some part of her. She felt like a child waiting for her dad to return home. A child so caught up playing games that he had been and gone. She missed his laughter, the takeaway pizzas and Marvel comic books.

When Angerstein entered the room, she hardly moved – she had become so insensitive that her natural instincts to cover up had been cast away as if natural selection had chosen her sexuality as a dominant trait. Only the strong survived in this world and her body was her weapon.

"Breakfast," said Angerstein.

"Thank you," said Eve, taking another sip from her cup.

Angerstein set a tray down next to her. It had a china plate with two pieces of buttered toast, a croissant and a pot of plum jam.

Eve picked up the croissant and took a bite. Crumbs fell from her lips onto the grass floor of the top floor apartment. She swallowed and looked at Angerstein, "Do you ever think about him?"

"Joshua?"

"Yes."

"All the time, but it is better this way. You're thinking about your dad?"

Eve nodded and brushed the crumbs from the top of her breasts, "You have my next assignment for me?"

"Hmm? Sorry I was–"

"Eyes on the job, Angerstein, you're a married man."

"I thought the rules of morality didn't apply to you?"

"I like you, okay?" said Eve. "In my world that means I don't want to fuck you."

Leaning forward she kissed him and then started applying the jam to her toast. Angerstein laughed, "You're a strange one, Eve."

Turning, he walked to the bed and sat down. "Servitude wants you to destroy Covenant's back-up systems, she has become too dangerous."

"And why does he need me? You can do that."

"Covenant's main weapon is her sexuality. You would be immune if you triggered her defence systems."

Angerstein passed Eve her white dressing gown, "And besides you were the one she confided in. She won't suspect you on a conscious level."

"Kill the bitch, eh?" said Eve. "Okay, it would be my pleasure."

"You have some jam on your lip," said Angerstein touching his own mouth.

"Sorry," said Eve. "Force of habit."

CHAPTER 6

Narrative disparity.

Prison.

Death row.

Hardly the place to be: far from the normality the brain craves and seeks. An end too horrible to contemplate – there has been a terrible mistake. Honestly. Listen for God's sake, this isn't supposed to happen. Please I live and breathe, I feel, I hope. I am not ready to go.

"Can you hold still, Vanity?"

I can feel my brain overriding what's happening. I am not here. I am not about to die. I'm not here, okay, "I am not here."

"Vanity, if you can control yourself then this will be far easier for all of us."

Static.

The sound of a pulse.

Blood flowing through veins, heart pumping.

"Lie still, Vanity."

"Servitude said to look for hidden memories connected with the terrorist attack on the Empire State Building."

"Yes, sir. We have been fully briefed, just relax."

I'm reading all this in a book. It's not real. God it feels so realistic and yet I am not here. I'm lying in bed next to my husband. The night-light is on. There is the sound of someone outside taking out the bins. No, I am at my keyboard typing this. Punching the letters on the keys. Stop.

S – t – o – p

I cannot; the story is an extension of me. I am the story.

Fade out into the white void.

"You are entering the Magnetic Resonance Imaging Core. It will record your approach to convergence. We are now administering the lethal injection. Please remain calm, we want a clean scan as you approach death."

The tip of a needle pierces skin. Something foreign enters my bloodstream. It itches, like falling through stinging nettles.

Have I lived so long for it to end like this?

I look up around me: a white inner chamber fills my view as I slide inside. There is nobody here except people in white coats to witness my departure. For this I risked everything. Where is Salient? I thought the Americans were on our side.

I am walking down the street in Durbuy past bluestone houses. What is that banging noise? I breathe in: inhale the sound and exhale the call of town bells. The street is cobbled. I can see Topiary Park. Castle spires form a majestic backdrop.

It's beautiful.

Rippling water, life flowing around clipped trees. I notice Antoine standing with Philippe waiting for me. I hesitate before threading my way past sculptures of ducks, people, an elephant: topiarian art over a hundred years old.

I pass a woman with clippers. She forms connections and allows shape to emerge as if she were a palaeontologist removing ancient soil to reveal prehistoric curiosities. Around me, cast iron lampposts leech rust from the sky.

I am drawn to the topiarist.

She looks up, smiles, says welcome and tells me her name is Covenant. She instructs me to lie still … I am in active retrieval. Soon things will speed up. She looks somehow familiar, but I can't place where I've seen her before.

And so I sit on the grass, watch my husband and child walk towards me. At first the clippers don't hurt, but when the topiarist severs my ears it starts to smart. I watch the blades coming together over my hair and strength ebbs away from the Delilahian cut. God it hurts. Flesh falls. It turns gold, blue and orange until I become a multitude of butterflies lifting into the air.

"She has started active retrieval."

"Memory extraction commencing."

…

"Do you like them? I made them to remind myself of when I was a little girl. The garden doesn't exist now."

"That's sad."

"Yes it is," I say and hold out my hand. A butterfly lands on the end of my finger. Faron copies me. Nothing happens. "I felt that part of my world had been taken from me," I say. "That I had faded slightly, my memories washed away by man and time." I turn to look at Faron, "Believe they will land on you and they will."

…

I'm in a garden as a little girl playing with my brother, Salient. My father, George is squirting water in my face, my mother is planting bulbs into the lawn. A table is set out with a pot of tea, scones piled high with jam and cream. Butterflies dance amongst the buddleia. My father picks me up, sets me down on a lavender blue chair. I smile as he pours me juice and passes me a scone.

And so I relive every moment of my life, each connected by random events as if my existence had no real meaning. The sense of déjà vu is almost overwhelming. The journey inward becomes a journey I believe is real. I am alive. I am sitting next to a man smiling at me. Words form on my dry lips causing him to smile, to shift towards me. His name is Antoine he tells me. Yes I know, I say, and then wonder how.

We make love. Afterwards I lie looking up at the ceiling. Fish are nibbling the lampshade.

…

I sigh and sit down next to Trent. The fish follow me and swim in and out of my hair. "Tell me about my father."

"There's nothing to say."

"I could bring him here from my memories, get him to ask you, ask you why you felt the need to kill him."

"No, please don't do that," says Trent, getting to his feet.

"Leaving?"

Trent turns and scowls at me, "Leave my son alone, if you harm him, I'll–"

"I can't die in my own dreamscape, Trent," I say. "Physically I'm thousands of miles away. How exactly would you stop me?"

"I'd find a way."
"Sit down, Richard."
…

Maybe Trent is behind all this now. Found a way all those years ago to lead me to this point. Is that possible? Someone has betrayed me, set me up, that's for sure.

But after a while the question I ask, the question everybody asks at some point in their life, is this:

Am I really here?

And before I can answer I live my life again. Each time my world becomes sweeter, connections that make sense form. The stories lose their lows, my father never leaves us. I enter a narrative that sees me achieve my hopes and dreams. My childhood garden still exists now, it lives and breathes in a jungle of industrial progress.

My story is complete. I cannot die.

"Memory retention approaching one hundred percent. Cycling at close to infinite speed. The singularity is starting to form."

"She's gone."

"Time of death: sixteen forty-five."

"Did we penetrate to any memories about the Empire State Building?"

"No, sir. There was nothing."

"Damn, she was good."

CHAPTER 7

ENGLAND: London: Hackney Central Post Office

Gabriel's last stand.

Gabriel was surrounded. The combined forces of pens, pencils, stickers and plastic rulers stood to Gabriel's left. Behind him, cheap plastic toys that lasted about as long as the drive back home. To his right: jars of fish paste, lighters for sale, birthday cards. Before him, the queue.

He planned to attack on three fronts.

To start with, he read the headlines on the newspapers stacked on the bottom shelf. Then he flipped through a top shelf magazine: porn taking the high ground from the politics and gossip filling newsprint below. That drew a few muttered complaints, especially when he turned the magazine and let the centrefold unfurl.

Finally: the full frontal attack. Gabriel tapped the person before him on the shoulder. The man wore a heavy jacket, needed the back of his neck shaving, wore 677 Chasse shoes.

"It's all worthless you know," said Gabriel. "Everything is pointless – you might as well give up now and go home."

"Excuse me?"

"I'd just go and have fun instead, forget about wasting your life standing here."

"Thanks, I've been here for twenty minutes: I'm not about to give up now."

"Who's the parcel for?"

The man frowned, "A word of advice my friend. The first rule of queuing in this country–" he paused. "You're not from around here are you?"

"No," said Gabriel.

"The first rule of queuing is, don't talk to other people in the queue."

"Right," said Gabriel. He took a chocolate bar from the middle shelf, pulled back the wrapper and took a bite.

"What are you doing?" said the man.

"I thought we couldn't–" Gabriel shoved the rest of the bar in his mouth, chewed, forced down the food. "Couldn't talk."

Gabriel scrunched up the aluminium foil, passed it between his hands a few times, then opened his palms outward. The wrapper had disappeared.

The man raised an eyebrow. Gabriel held up his finger indicating he just needed a moment then, reaching forward into the man's coat pocket, he pulled out the wrapper.

Gabriel winked, put it to his lips, blew hard, showed that the wrapper was now filled with the chocolate bar again, the seal reformed. Smiling, Gabriel placed it back on the shelf.

The man's eyes opened wide, shaking his head he said, "Look, just leave me alone," and faced forward again.

Gabriel conceded defeat at that point and went home.

Once there, he got a jar of powdered green tea down from the cupboard. Scooping some into a steel sieve, he placed a smooth stone from the Sabinal River on top of it. He shook it for a moment and smelt cut hay as the fine powder fell in the air. Then he placed the matcha in a tea bowl and added hot water.

Settling down on his tatami mat, he began to watch daytime television. After a few minutes he became bored and gazed instead at the mist drifting past the bamboo outside his window.

Worthless, he thought. Meaningless, when will they see that everything comes to nothing. Their minds seeking stories in their lives in the same way their brains are conditioned to look for faces in patterns.

The phone rang.

Gabriel ignored it.

After all what was the point?

CHAPTER 8

USA: Houston: Houston National Cemetery

Bathsheba's father held the black umbrella over her head, shielding her from the battering rain. Behind them the imposing bell tower of the Hemicycle, before them honour guards in full military uniform carrying the casket draped in the flag of The United States of America.

"Why does it always rain at funerals?" said Bathsheba.

"It's the Lord showing you that he cares," said her father.

Members of Uriah's battalion saluted as the casket passed them.

"You're not really going to get married to Reagan are you?"

"Not now, Dad," said Bathsheba. "Why do we always have to be arguing?"

"He's four times your age."

"He's the president of our country."

The sound of blanks from M16 rifles rang out as the three-volley salute began. The American and Texas Lone Star flags fell limp as the wind dropped.

"Sorry, love," said Bathsheba's father. "I just want the best for my little girl."

Bathsheba moved her hand over her swollen stomach. "He's going to love his Grandad."

"When do you move into the White House?"

"I don't know, Dad. After we're married I guess."

"And he couldn't make it here today?"

"Don't you think this is awkward enough for him?"

The tune, Day is Done, played by the lone bugler, mixed with the patter of raindrops on the road. Moonlight lit up the semi-circular monument wrapped around the scene.

A soldier from the honour guard stepped forward, knelt and presented Bathsheba with the flag from the coffin, neatly folded: three shell cases within.

"Please accept this flag as a symbol of our appreciation for your loved one's honourable and faithful service."

She smiled and burst into tears.

CHAPTER 9

"Clone?"

"Yes, how did you know?" said Lemaître.

"You have *Convergence Clone* stamped in black on the back of your prison uniform."

"So do you."

"No," she laughed. "I'm not a clone, I'm a regular human being."

"Well it says *Convergence Clone* on your back."

"You're kidding me, right?"

"Bienvenue au club," said Lemaître.

"No there's been a mistake, my name is Vanity, I'm here because your government thinks I'm a terrorist."

"Did you find it strange that you could recall every detail of your life when they were interrogating you?"

"Well–"

"And your life has just been one wonderful story after another – nothing bad has ever happened – you've never cried, had your heart broken, lost a loved one?"

"Well, yes, but that's my faith," said Vanity. "God has guided me and protected me."

"No, you're definitely a Convergence Clone. Sorry to be the one to break it to you."

"No, I'm not a clone, they're not real people. I'm a real person. I should know. "

"I heard that after they've finished with you they pulp you down to reuse your substrate."

"Listen," said Vanity, "do you think you could stop talking?"

The door to the cell opened. A prison guard stepped in and beckoned, "Lemaître, it's time to go."

"Mademoiselle," whispered Lemaître. "Make your peace with that God of yours, you don't have long."

"Shut up," shouted the guard. Bringing his baton down, he broke Lemaître's legs. The rats on the floor scattered, the noise of crying flowed down the corridor. In the sluice on the floor: blood, a finger nail, hair, teeth.

CHAPTER 10

CROATIA: Dubrovnik: Church of St. Blaise

"Bless me, Father, for I have sinned. It has been three years since my last confession."

The priest looked at his watch. Dust suspended in the air swirled over the clock face. Blue hands moved closer to five-o'clock.

"Given the time, my son, I think your confession can wait until another day."

"Please, Father."

Shafts of light pierced the confessional chamber, at first solid and then flickering as the low light from the moon swept past the swaying branches of the newly planted trees in the square. The twilight found a frequency that brought the dust to a standstill – the priest's watch stopped ticking. He tapped it, brought it to his ear.

"My sins are many, Father. I haven't watched Ask the Family for six months."

"Yes, yes," said the priest. "And you wish forgiveness."

He wound his watch, its mechanical heart pumped and clicked but the hands remained frozen. The priest closed his eyes, counted numbers that found no end, "Do you have the time?"

"It's a minute to five-o'clock, Father. Is that a problem?"

"Well yes, of course," said the priest. "We will have to end here."

"I can pay," said the man.

"Can you indeed," said the priest, gathering his robes as he rose to his feet. The noise of rats eating old bones under the floor floated up. It sounded like frozen leaves crunching under feet.

"You have a deposit," said the priest's monetary implant. "Value two million dollars."

The priest diverted the money to the Family Protection Agency Memorial Fund.

"You," said the man, "are now in violation of the Protection of Families Act and as such I sentence you to death in accordance with the law."

"You said it was a minute to five," said the priest.

"I lied."

"That's entrapment," said the priest sitting back down.

"You have still broken the law," said the man appearing at the curtain before the priest's chamber. "You will come with me." He flashed his Family Protection Agency badge.

"For fuck's sake," said the priest, resting his head in his hands.

"Get up," said the man kicking the priest with his boot.

"Sadness bleaches the heart," said the priest. "Makes it sterile. I no longer desire the comfort of a woman. I no longer love. I no longer fear. I no longer hate."

The man pulled a gun from his jacket and pointed it at the priest's head. The smell of the priest's old wooden chair rose up into the dome above. The gold-plated statue of St. Blasius glowed in the moonlight. A candle went out. The marble altars dropped in temperature.

The priest sighed, raised himself up.

"That's better."

"I will give you five minutes start," said the priest.

"Excuse me?"

"Okay, six then," said the priest. "After that I will kill you and feed you to the rats in the harbour. You dare enter here and entrap me with the most sacred of laws? A law she lost her life upholding."

"Okay," said the man. "Have it your way." He pulled the trigger.

The bullet left the end of the gun. It slowed as if the air had become layer after layer of paper folded to ensnare the projectile in an origami maze. The bullet stopped and floated between the priest and the enforcement agent.

"That's five minutes now," said the priest. "I'd start running if I were you."

"Velocity suspension envelope holding at one hundred per cent, Pete," said Covenant in the priest's audio implant.

The agent raised an eyebrow, his gaze fixed on the moonlit bullet spinning before him.

"Actually," said the priest, "I've rather changed my mind. I'll just shoot you now if you don't mind." Reaching forward he took the gun with a quick turn of his wrist.

The man's eyes widened. In their curvature: the priest, the confessional chamber, baroque architecture waiting for the chosen to return, the barrel of his gun.

BLAM!

"Shall I arrange for the body to be removed, Pete?" asked Covenant.

"You shouldn't have used my name," said Pete making the sign of the cross over his priestly robes. "You forced my hand. I had no choice but to kill him."

"It is written," said Covenant, "that a man should not–"

"I'm not in the mood, Covenant," said Pete. "I've just killed a man after hours – isn't that how it all started for Trent?"

"Very good, Pete."

"Did you send him here?"

"What a strange question," said Covenant.

"Did you? And are you responsible for this?" Pete held his wrist up to show his watch.

"Can you step aside," said Covenant.

"What?"

"The suspension envelope is decaying, the bullet is about to carry on and rip through your chest."

Pete reached out, took hold of the bullet and placed it in his mouth, "Did you send that corrupt enforcement agent here?"

"Now, Peter," said Covenant. "Take the bullet out of your mouth."

"I don't trust you," said Pete. He stepped over the body avoiding the pool of blood. "How can I be sure you have truly changed sides?"

"Peter, darling. Have we not saved many from their sins?"

"I'm ending all this right now," said Pete. "I was only doing it for her. For her memory. How many months now have I prayed and fasted imploring God to bring an end to the sin that rots the family? And yet you bring violence to me, here where I find sanctuary from my old life. Am I not holy now as she was?"

"The suspension field will fail in thirty seconds, Peter."

"I have broken my most sacred promise not to work overtime."

"Peter!"

Pete opened his arms out and turned his palms upwards. "I come now, Father, to be with her again. To join her."

"Peter!"

"Our Father, who art in heaven," Pete closed his eyes. "Hallowed be thy Name." He felt the bullet on his tongue, "Thy kingdom come." He thought of the blood within him that would not stop flowing once he was pierced, "Thy will be done–"

Pete thought of her. He could see the glare of hospital lights, hear water spiralling down a basin, a girl laughing. He started to swallow.

"Peter," said Covenant. "Durram is alive. Stop this. She lives. Trent killed a clone of her. She is alive."

At the sound of her name:

Flowers blew across the sea,

a rush of blood in the storm.

Soil became fertile ground,

overlain with gold.

Pete's pupils dilated. Within them, the image of an old grey man walking up the staircase, his weight on his staff.

Pete spat the bullet out. It fell towards the floor then, before it hit, flew off and embedded itself in the stone wall behind him. A puff of dust floated down from the impact.

"What? What are you talking about?"

"Durram was cloned when she was in the amniotic fluid tank having her legs grown back. Servitude knew Trent was going to kill her and so released the clone enabling the real Durram to enter covert operations."

"What! Where is she?"

"America."

"Excuse me," said the old man before him now.

Pete looked at him. He had a long beard, his face not unlike the statue to his side.

"What?"

"Excuse me, but we are in great danger. The end of all things is coming. You must act."

"Not now, old man," said Pete. "I need to book a plane ticket."

CHAPTER 11

USA: Texas: Medina Lake

Nestled up in the wood, near the edge of Medina Lake: a black London cab, door open, its orange taxi sign shining out into the Texas night.

Before the taxi driver: the large dam irrigating Medina Valley. A valley full of cows after Reagan signed bill S.261907, nicknamed the John Wayne Act, to return America to its past glory of cattle farming and cowboys.

The taxi driver stubbed out his cigarette, behind him the sticker *I Hate Cows*. He'd gotten the idea to blow up the dam after watching The Masked Rider. Piled up on the back seat were boxes of dynamite. The trip from London across Europe, the barren wastelands of Russia and the Bering Strait Bridge had nearly killed him. He'd frozen half to death, been shot at by Americans at the border controls around Russia and lost an arm to a polar bear.

Panting, his breath misting in the air, he pulled out a shotgun and stepped onto the earth. The cows had spread like a plague. There was even a cow here, despite the sheer drop from the pale rocks to the lake below. The taxi driver rested the shotgun on top of the open door, took aim.

"I hate fucking cows," he muttered.

The cow was pointing away, showing its pink udders. It turned to face him. It reminded the taxi driver of the cover to Pink Floyd's Atomic Heart Mother.

"Back to Mama," said the taxi driver and pulled the trigger.

The bullet entered the cow's lung. The animal stumbled backward, slid off the edge and plummeted to the waters below. There was an almighty splash and then it sank, rear first, through a swirl of water taking it past carp, bass, catfish. A puff of silt ballooned up on impact with the riverbed. The vibrations travelled down through a mile of limestone and reached a concrete dome forming part of the foundations to the dam. Within it was artificial lighting, heat, the hum of machines, the smell of humans, the chatter of voices, the newly activated clone of the president of the United States of America. The impact of the cow above sent a puff of dust down from the ceiling.

"So this is the assassin that killed me?" said Reagan brushing the dust from his suit.

"Yes, Mr President. Her name is Durram Brittle."

"Strange name. Did I die well?"

"You saluted, sir, a loyal American to the end."

"How many clones of me do we have left?"

"You are the last one until we get more funding, Mr President."

"Excuse me," said a man in a white coat. "The Addams Family is starting, if you don't want to miss the start, I'd come now."

Reagan smiled, rubbed his hands, "Oh, goody."

"I think we can stream that to you later, Mr President, I need to brief you on the Convergence Project. We need your permission to use Durram."

"Why?"

"She's a British citizen, so we'd need The Chief of Staff's permission. Protocol dictates in the event of his death that that authority passes to the President."

"But this is the episode where we get to find out Uncle Fester's surname."

"He hasn't got a surname, Mr President."

"Don't be silly, man, everyone's got a surname. I mean you for example are ... are –"

"Mr Dawson, Mr President."

"Of course, Mr Dawson."

BLEEP. BLEEP. BLEEP.

Durram opened her eyes for a moment. She felt weightless, saw the image of a huge tree growing up over her head. Voices talking...

"What's happening?" said Reagan.

51

"I er ... What's happening?" said Dawson to a man in a white coat.

"We can't hold onto her much longer. She's inflicted a critical wound to herself. If we are to do this, then it has to be now."

"Mr President?" said Dawson.

"What would I be agreeing to?" asked Reagan. He looked at Durram. She lay at the mouth of the machine awaiting insertion. The newly-formed clone of Durram floated in a suspension tank next to his right shoulder. Reagan tapped the glass, watched the bubbles stream upwards. The clone was edged in a blue glow. Wires projected out of its body.

"Hang on," said Dawson. He walked over to a glass unit attached to the wall. On it a message in red letters ...

Eat in case of emergency.

Dawson smashed the glass and reaching in through the crushed ice brought out a sandwich wrapped in shrink plastic.

"This will speed things up."

"You know how I hate those things," said Reagan. "They seem so foreign – are you sure there's no Ruskie tech in there?"

"Quite sure, Mr President."

"What flavour is it?"

"Chicken, sir."

Reagan opened the sandwich, started eating.

"If you could be quick, Mr President."

"I'm doing the best I can. Can you get me a drink of Coke to get this down?"

Durram closed her eyes. What was going on? She was aware of the tree – how could she not be – it was so beautiful. And for some reason the man she had killed now stood before her eating a sandwich. Durram could hear the alarms sounding around the room. She felt faint, giddy, sick to her very core. As she stared upwards, her view became filled by a large white dome. She was moving. Moving into the heart of the machine.

Reagan took the glass and downed the last of his sandwich. Wiping the crumbs from his suit, he closed his eyes …

Data Entry Device: Sandwich

Filling: Chicken

Classification: Top Secret – Level 5

Subject: The Convergence Project

Saliva: Authorisation match

…

Do you wish to synch?

"Yes," said Reagan.

The information encoded into the DNA of the chicken sandwich synched with Reagan's DNA. In the very fabric of his being Reagan knew all there was to know about The Convergence Project – he didn't even have to think about it – he just knew, in much the same way his old heart knew it should keep beating. For now anyway.

It was bold. He'd give them that. If not highly immoral. Durram started screaming. He should probably make a decision. What was it Nancy used to say? Go with your gut feeling. She'd laugh now Reagan thought, the sandwich swilling within his stomach. Not that she had ever laughed at any of his jokes. Still. He had forgiven her. He was sure of that. Wasn't he? They were good jokes. Especially the one about the Russians. My fellow Americans. I'm pleased to announce that I've signed legislation outlawing the Soviet Union. We begin bombing in five minutes. Reagan laughed. Dawson raised an eyebrow.

So, The Convergence Project, he should focus on that, block out the panic around him, the screaming. God, when was she going to shut up? Shut up woman. For God's sake, you do drone on. Reagan shook his head: his mind confusing his feelings towards Nancy with the screaming of Durram.

Focus.

He was the President of The United States of America.

The Convergence Project …

The experience of life flashing before your eyes just before death is a process called active retrieval where memories are being recalled and lived out again in the mind.

As the amount of time before death decreases, the brain exponentially increases the speed of playback and starts looping: repeating, over and over, a lifetime's worth of memories. Each playback makes the memories stronger and retains more detail.

Mathematically you can always halve the remaining time before death – so one second to death becomes half a second to death then a quarter of a second and so on to a billionth of a second, a trillionth, until finally the memories are being replayed over and over in an infinitesimally small amount of time before death. As the brain exponentially increases the speed of playback at each iteration and there is no end to this process, an infinite playback speed is reached, forming a memory singularity called a Convergence Point.

Definition: Convergence Point – a lifetime's worth of memories contained within an infinitesimally small amount of time.

Theory:

1 – The consciousness is editing the memories to form a memory timeline that is acceptable to the brain before the Convergence Point is reached.

2 – When, in the last moments, a person is in a Convergence Point then, from their perspective, as their brain is processing at an infinite speed, that 'moment' lasts for ever and they effectively enter an afterlife of their own making.

Testing: Subjects on death row are killed by lethal injection within an enhanced Magnetic Resonance Imaging Core. This brings on active retrieval and the brain activity is imaged moments before the Convergence Point forms. So far the project has failed to image a Convergence Point itself as it disappears exactly at the moment it comes into being, although the project can get close to it. These 'near' Convergence Points are downloaded into neutral clones – this being the most effective way of interacting with the data as the clone effectively decodes the brain patterns back into memories. These 'Convergence Clones' are subjected to psychoanalysis to try to gain an understanding of the death experience. In particular to investigate how the subject interacted with the memories to form narratives to their lives. It is also noted that this method produces far superior clone matching than does the normal memory transfer sequencing method.

Reagan's mind drifted back to Bathsheba in the pool at the Ubud Hanging Gardens. He imagined her being lifted up, drops of water falling from her toes. He moved her out over the forest and held her there above the canopy. The edges of her skin blurred into the green backdrop until she became at one with it and disappeared.

Reagan pulled himself back to the project ...

The project has the added bonus of extracting information held deep in the subconscious of terrorists by using Convergence on them and then interrogating their Convergence Clone, which is then recycled after use and reformed.

The project is government funded in partnership with the Covenant Foundation which provides the advanced AI interface.

"Okay," said Reagan. "There's potential for some good jokes–"

"It's top secret, Mr President," said Dawson.

"Yes well, always a spoilsport eh, Dawson? Okay do it, I want to find out who sent her to kill me."

Dawson turned and motioned to the men in white coats.

They nodded and pushed some buttons.

Durram clenched her fists then relaxed as she watched the breeze filter through the leaves of the tree towering over her. It grew up through the roof, entwining within the concrete. It seemed so real. The tree lifted up, punching through the room, roots ripping through the floor, dirt falling, pinning her down, entering her mouth.

She couldn't breathe.

Branches snagged at the wires surrounding her and pushed through her clothes until she could feel roots piercing her skin, puncturing her, bleeding her. In her mind she lifted upwards into the sky: taken by the ascension of the tree, embraced within it on a journey out of this world.

"Why is she screaming so loudly?" asked Reagan.

"She could be hallucinating," said Dawson. "She has traces of Avodah in her bloodstream. Maybe that's affecting her."

"Avodah?"

"It's an illegal drug used by the CIA. It slows the perception of time by increasing processing speeds in the brain with glutamate."

"Well, whatever," said Reagan, "can you get them to shut her up?"

"Of course, sir."

Needles entered Durram's arms.

Reagan tapped a light on a console. It occurred to him that perhaps he himself was a Convergence Clone – why else had they awakened him here? In fact when he thought about it his memories were rather polished as if they'd been edited and spliced together. There were no loose ends, everything in his life seemed to have resolved itself rather well: an Oscar for a Kings Row with his immortal line, "Where's the rest of me?"; receiving the Nobel Peace Prize for his attacks against the evil of communism; and sex with Nancy had always been spectacular. Odd.

"Dawson, a moment please."

"Sir?"

"Am I one of these Convergence Clone things?"

"Yes, sir, it boosts performance, gives you a deeper sense of well-being."

"But we didn't have this tech in the eighties did we?"

"No, you're not a direct descendent from the original – we had to use a normal clone as a starting point and work from its life experiences."

"So you managed to get the previous clone in this thing," Reagan pointed at the machine, "before I – or it died from the gunshot wound?"

"Yes, Mr President, before you died."

"Of the gunshot wound?"

"Of the gunshot wound."

"Which was fatal?"

"Well technically, no sir, but we thought it for the best."

Reagan stared at Dawson for a moment. They had killed his previous clone in the machine rather than risk losing him.

"I'm off to watch The Addams family," he said finally. "Let me know what you discover."

Durram relaxed and felt the vastness of the sky tug at her sense of wonder. A gentle breeze caressed the branches of the tree. The clanging noises of the MRI machine faded, blanketing the scene in reflective slumber. The sun slipped under the horizon. Orange and pale yellow glows washed around the impression left in the sky. The evening colours flowed down to follow the warmth, striating the sky into darkening blues. Images of stars across the horizon twinkled in her eyes as she watched the darkness claim the stage. For a moment the memory of Pete surfaced and spoke to her in whispers but, when she turned to look at him, she saw instead the image of a woman.

"Welcome, Durram, I've been waiting for you."

"Waiting?"

"Oh yes," said the topiarist raising up her clippers. "And so it ends, as all things must eventually end."

"She has started active retrieval."

"Memory extraction commencing."

Déjà vu.

…

Officer Durram Deep looked through her gun sights and framed the blurred image in the cross-hairs.

"Keep her steady, Pete."

Durram watched as the digital enhancer gave the image shape, and President John F. Kennedy appeared. Hacked into the normal schedule by the Overtime Underground Network, the black and white propaganda film showed images of Kennedy giving his 1962 speech stating his intentions to have Americans walk on the moon before the end of the decade. Durram scanned across and settled on a man standing in front of the television wall. Layers of information stacked up between the bullet in Durram's gun chamber and the man before her. The movement of soot particles blown from north of the river, the motion of a magpie gliding before glass refracting evening light.

…

"She's processing much faster than normal."

"Could be the traces of Avodah in her bloodstream. It may be compromising the procedure."

"Should we be concerned?"

"No, it may even increase the quality of the Convergence Point."

...

She'd talk to Pete tonight – ask him the question. Turning, she walked back to the man she had killed, the smell of blood like rust, the smell of the inanimate. When would these people learn she thought, the family was sacred, pure, a thing of beauty in a world of commerce and greed.

...

Durram rose out of her memories like a diver coming up for air. She gasped, returned.

...

She was back in the garage forecourt at the moment of the explosion. For a moment she was everywhere: the furnace of stars, the cold embrace of the moon, the cry of a child. She watched as humanity collapsed into a single point and became nothing, pointless, worthless as if everything that had ever passed was only vanity maintaining the illusion of meaning.

...

At the point of reliving the pain of losing her legs, her mind snapped and returned to the tree. It was part of her and she of it. This was her past. She rejected her own memories and, treating them as foreign bodies, accepted instead the world of Avodah...

The bark is a skin weathered by sun, wind, rain, snow. A history of time marked out as the tree orbits the sun. Around the pith, rings growing ever outward like the planetary halo of a large planet. Its heartwood stronger than iron, rising water in its sapwood bringing life from soil to stars.

"Memory retention approaching one hundred percent. Cycling at close to infinite speed. Something is wrong. Her brain activity is unlike anything we have ever seen before."

"Stop it. Pull her out."

A canopy of mottled greens encircle the tree, a wood without end: the white froth of clouds dancing upon them. Rivers below flowing like liquid gold in the dappled sunlight. Questions thrown as seeds into the wind looking for soil to take root, to explain, to answer: why?

"The singularity is starting to form."

In the air around the tree are the sounds of stories diffused into heart beats, rhythms left over from words. The folly of man looking for understanding held by roots in ancient earth. What endures is woven into the landscape: beauty, love, hope, connection.

"Memory retention at one hundred percent. Cycling at infinite speed. The singularity has formed."
"What? We've captured it?"

Man, fire, machines, hate, violence; all pound at the door wanting to be let in. Doctrinal keys fail in locks that respond only to the voices of those woven into narratives: the story is everything. And everything will become the story.

CHAPTER 12

At first it appeared like a small soap bubble as the magnetic field density shifted. Flashes of light darted between the forming orb and the inner casing of the machine. It was beautiful: as if the blue star in Orion was glowing above Durram's head.

She opened her eyes, looked out with a blank stare. The orb grew in size. The scientists stepped forward, watching as it expanded until Durram's head was completely inside. It added a blue hue to everything within, like a filter applied by a photographer to enhance a scene and make the mundane appear magical. Indeed to the scientists, Durram's face now seemed younger, her eyes glistening, her lips fuller.

"Amazing! What are we looking at?"

"I'm not sure. Perhaps the Convergence Point has a physical embodiment – somehow, in observing the process, we have changed something – caused the probability of its location to collapse to reveal it."

"I hope not – being in her mind is one thing – but here, now, in front of us? The singularity would distort our space time. Nothing would escape."

"It's still expanding."

"I'm not sure you should touch it."

Bird song flowed out from the sphere, the air in the lab became sweeter, the moisture content increased. Expanding, it encompassed the machine. Durram sat up slowly as if she were performing in a Japanese musical drama. She looked around at the room, stared at her clone floating in the tube. Swinging her legs off the table, she started to stand up.

"Remarkable," said the scientist, "Durram can you hear us?"

He reached forward and touched the sphere.

His fingertips disappeared. Then as the orb grew, his fingers, knuckles and hand.

"What the –?"

The scientist stepped back, blood gushed from the stump where his hand had been, the orb pushed into his side. For a moment it appeared as if someone had erased one half of him in a flowing arc. Then he was gone. Durram rose up and floated in the centre of the sphere, her hands outstretched, her hair billowing. The machine distorted and became the roots of a large tree. They grew and wove around her.

"Get back," shouted Dawson. He hit the alarm. Metal shutters came down, a red glow filled the room, a siren sounded.

CHAPTER 13

Vanity's convergence clone watched the blue glow in the corridor. She had accepted it now. It made sense. When she thought back, it did seem odd that her memory of her childhood garden still existed even though it was surrounded by industrial warehouses. Why would that survive when everything else had been knocked down? She had seen it as a sign from God, a miracle: an oasis of beauty in a world stained by the vanity of man seeking progress.

Now it seemed the memory was false, a fabrication of her dying mind. But did it matter? What was real anyway? Everything was just her senses interpreting the world, making sense of it all so she could function; her brain perceiving meaning in images, changing the world into patterns and narratives without any conscious consent. She couldn't interact directly with reality, only reconstruct it within her mind. That was the beauty of the dreamscape she so loved inhabiting: a projection of her mind, it formed a closer connection than reality ever could.

She could hear screaming, shouting from the cells near hers.

Silence.

When the orb came, its envelope expanded into her cell with such serenity she didn't know how to react. Her senses confused by its grace and beauty. And so when she stepped into it she felt no alarm, no pain or fear, no surge of adrenalin. Just a deep sense of peace, of freedom, of flying.

CHAPTER 14

The riff of a harpsichord and the sound of snapped fingers filled the room. BEWARE OF THE THING. Reagan smiled, took a slurp of Coke, munched some popcorn.

Lurch: "Follow me."

Reagan watched as Lurch slid open large doors to reveal Mr Addams.

The lights suddenly came on in the cinema to the sound of canned laughter. Reagan shielded his eyes. Ten armed men raced in and surrounded him.

"Mr President," said their leader. "There has been a situation. We need to evac you right now."

"What's happening, are the Ruskies attacking?"

"Sir, we must get you out of here now. Follow me."

The soldier made towards the exit then stopped.

Before him, the curvature of the orb pushed into the room. Reagan looked at it. It appeared transparent. Within he could see Durram half cocooned within the roots of a great tree as if she were an inner flower within a dandelion's ring of bracts. The soldiers formed a wall before Reagan and pointed their guns at the growing sphere.

"Aim for the woman," said the soldier in charge.

"Is there no other way out?" said Reagan backing away, his feet squashing popcorn strewn across the floor.

"No, sir."

To the side of them, The Addams Family continued to play...

Lurch: "You rang?"

The noise of gunfire filled the cinema.

Uncle Fester: "Yes, Lurch, what's going on?"

The bullets blinked out of existence as they hit the edge of the orb.

Reagan watched as the sphere engulfed the soldiers. Moving backwards he made for the back seats, sat down, watched. Perhaps this was for the best, he thought. He didn't know what would happen, the soldiers just seemed to have disappeared, there was no sign of them within the sphere. So if this was it, if he was about to die, then to be honest it was a blessed relief – he was fed up with being cloned all the time – they had killed the last clone of him just to protect his memories. Stuck a needle in his arm and shoved him in that machine. And he was fed up with being the President of The United States of America – the hours were long, no nine to five for him, constant photo shoots with bloody cows and half the world hated him.

Arh, well. He picked up a piece of popcorn from the floor, ate it, heard Uncle Fester reveal his name, stood to his feet to the sound of incidental music, saluted. When, in his last moment, he finally remembered Bathsheba and his unborn child, he panicked and died with his back pressed against the wall.

CHAPTER 15

The explosion from the dynamite ripped a hole in the dam, sending water gushing down into Medina Valley. The taxi driver jumped up and punched the air, "Take that you bloody cows!"

He got back into his cab, turned on the ignition and started backing away. His mission was complete, he'd go back to the Travelodge and watch the carnage play out on the news channel. Maybe order in a pizza. It would be cow armageddon, they'd probably make a film about him. He was a fucking hero.

He flicked on the lights, then stopped. His cigarette fell from his lips and dropped to the floor. In the middle of the lake, illuminated in the headlights, was a huge vortex of water. A white glow deep below it brought memories of childhood books on the evidence for extra-terrestrials. He recalled thinking as a boy, what would he do if he ever had a close encounter with aliens: go with them, or blow them to bits? Blow them to bits. He reached over for his shotgun and stepped out of the cab.

As he got closer to the edge he could see that hardly any of the water was entering the valley. Although the dam was breached the water was draining into the middle of the lake and forming the vortex. It was if someone had pulled a plug out: the water level was dropping.

"No!" shouted the taxi driver. He started firing into the lake. "No, no, no."

A moment later he was looking at a dry lakebed. Fish flapped in the silt struggling to breathe, a few had gunshot wounds.

Silence.

No extra-terrestrials.

It was him. Somehow he had triggered it. What had he done? He was only supposed to blow the damned thing up.

He decided to run, to get back to England. He'd be safe there.

Reaching his cab, he turned the ignition.

There was no response.

He turned the key again and thumped the dash with his fist. The figurine of Jesus balanced on top of a spring wobbled like a Hawaiian dancer.

"Damn."

He got out, opened the boot and started putting his Coke bottle collection into a carrier bag. He had fifty-six so far, all with the name of Michelle on them, the names a marketing ploy to establish intimacy with the consumer. He'd been collecting them on the journey – every time choosing the ones with Michelle on. He had never known a Michelle but had formed a bond with the woman he imagined her to be and there was no way he was leaving her behind.

And so he left, running back into the trees with Michelle or a herd of Michelles at his side.

Behind him, the top of the orb pushed out of the lakebed, rewriting reality, bringing a woodland floor, worms, bluebells, Durram. The cocoon opened and fell away, leaving her on freshly-formed soil, wet, moist, and damp. Next to her a stump started to form.

The taxicab's headlights streamed forward towards Durram's world and stopped at the boundary. And in the dark of the night the sunlit scene within shone brightly, like a star.

CHAPTER 16

ENGLAND: Hackney: Work Conditioning Building

"And how many hours a week would you be looking for?"

"I don't mind."

The man looked up, "I have to have a figure."

"Fifty hours a week."

"That would be highly illegal, as well you know," said the man, pushing the alarm button under the desk. "I'll put you down for the maximum allowance of thirty hours."

"As you wish."

"And what kind of work would you be looking for?"

"Anything really. I've done just about every job under the sun, and I can tell you it is all utterly meaningless – a chasing after the wind."

"Is that so? And how is it then that you are claiming benefits and not working now?"

"As I said I've really tried everything and I just can't find anything that satisfies."

"You've tried everything?"

"Yes, well I've been around for rather a long time."

"Well you won't mind waiting in that queue there then. When you get to the front, hand in these forms."

"Thank you," said Gabriel. "In the meantime can you pay my allowance straight into your own private account."

"What?"

"I don't want the money. What would I need money for? You on the other hand have recently defaulted on your mortgage and can't afford new school shoes for your kid."

"How do you know that?"

"Lucky guess."

"Listen, are you deliberately trying to wind me up, or are you just a complete nutter?"

Gabriel coughed, "Excuse me I think I have something in the back of my throat." He spluttered, held his stomach, puffed his cheeks out and held up his finger to signal the man wait a moment.

"What?"

Gabriel coughed again, then opened his mouth. A fifty dollar bill floated out and landed on the desk. Gabriel smiled, got to his feet and held out his arms. A multitude of dollar bills flew out of his sleeves and swirled up into the air. The people in the queue behind him leapt up and started snatching the money. Gabriel laughed, fell over backwards and lay on the oatmeal carpet tiles moving his arms and legs up and down as if he were in snow.

The dollar bills floated down into people's eager arms. Chaos, people fighting, laughing, shouting, doors bursting open: Family Protection Agents.

The interviewer motioned to Gabriel and, within seconds, Gabriel found himself surrounded, the Agents' guns pointing inwards towards him like the spokes of a wheel.

CHAPTER 17

CROATIA: Dubrovnik: The Walls of Dubrovnik

I twist my heart slowly,
leaving my body numb.
It hurts less that way,
the slow release as she fades away.

The terracotta tiles of the city of Dubrovnik jostled towards the stone walls dividing man from the clear blue waters. Pete imagined himself running over the red roofs, jumping from house to house on a voyage to the sea. The past behind him like a silent assailant watching: a predator waiting to strike, to bring him to account.

He'd made this his home, this city restored from the ravages of earth and man. It had served him well – brought a freedom. The Croatian limestone paving the streets bringing a simple beauty and strength, the same stone underpinning Venice and rising in white columns at The White House.

When he first arrived at Dubrovnik he'd cared for nothing. Tired of life, he had thought of jumping to his death – to be dashed on the dragon scales of limestone, to tumble into the Adriatic. Dubrovnik in the end though had healed him, its simple life, the absence of milk-guzzling cars, the lack of signs in the Stradun keeping the mystery alive. And here he had found a peace, a way of living that enabled him to battle in prayer the sins of a work-obsessed society. Covenant had helped him form an identity as the local priest, showed him spiritual weapons: faith, truth and honesty.

Pete thought of Durram, imagined her standing beside him, her hand finding his, their lives as one. His last moment with her had been with her hands around his throat. Throttling, strangling, hurting. He thought of the curve of her cheek, the line of her nose, the way her hair fell over her eyes. She had shaped his thinking, his belief system; she was as much a part of him as this city was part of the rock that rose up out of the sea. But he was afraid if Durram rejected him again, he would crumble to dust, that history would crush him and bring a balance.

And there was the old man in the church appearing out of nowhere, uttering nonsense about the end of the world. Perhaps he was needed? Maybe there was a reason for everything.

Pete made his way to the cable car that the tourists so loved, and paid for his ticket. It was a ridiculous amount of effort to make a phone call, however the only way to get a signal was to ride the car to the top of Srdj.

Inside, an old couple were huddled in the corner in their winter coats. Pete smiled but they seemed unaware of him and were deep in their own world, years in the making. He could just hear them as they ascended encased in glass.

"The flowers are so lovely in the garden, don't you think, George?" said the old woman, her hands caught in an arthritic cage.

"They are lovely, a little splash of colour in our world of tea and cake."

"And knitting."

"And knitting," said George placing his weight on his oak walking stick.

"Do you fancy a fuck at the top?" said the old woman.

"Yes that would be lovely," said George.

Pete smiled to himself and looked at Lokrum Island. He dreamed of restoring the Benedictine monastery and setting up home there with Durram. It could be a place where they could grow old together surrounded by paradise. Below him trees replaced the terracotta, then barren rock. Towards the top his audio implant picked up a signal and made the call.

"Hello?"

"Servitude?"

"Yes, who is this?"

"It's Pete, Chief."

"Pete, what the hell are you doing ringing me?"

"Durram is alive."

"What?"

"I know all about your involvement with the Overtime Underground Network," said Pete, "Covenant told me."

"Covenant?"

"Why else didn't people search for Trent at Tamarisk in the first place?" Pete asked. "You protected him until – what? Sorry, yes I'll talk quieter."

"Who was that?"

"Just a sweet old couple, don't worry. You protected him until Covenant blew the whistle."

"Now listen, Pete–"

"You knew of the plan to kill Durram."

"I was playing for higher stakes, Pete. The Overtime Underground network was a joke, but it suited us to use them to gain access to the Americans. You must know that it is always about the Americans."

"Why didn't you tell me she was alive?"

"Pete, that was classified information, you are just a helicopter pilot for God's sake."

"You allowed me to, to–"

"Pete, what do you mean Covenant told you. Is she with you?"

"Yes, she's swapped sides. She's helping me."

"Now listen very carefully, Pete. You are not to trust Covenant, okay?"

"Why not?"

"Why not? Pete are you a complete idiot? She's using you."

"Right."

"And stay away from Durram, officially she's dead. I don't want you storming in there and blowing her cover."

"Right."

Pete stepped out of the cable car and looked across at the cross set into the rock. Behind him the old couple made their way arm in arm towards the hotel their movement slow and stiff as if Ray Harryhausen were keeping them alive by the magic of stop motion. Pete breathed in the mixture of sea and mountain air, tried to calm himself. He thought of her, how she was like a pool: deep, clear and crystal that went on forever. It had been almost a decade ago – she was probably a different person now. He wondered if she still thought of him, if he filled her mind as she did his every day. Why had she never tried to contact him, let him know she was alive? Perhaps it was best not to risk unravelling his heart, perhaps if he found her he would be pierced for his transgressions.

"Pete?"

"I'm not coming back, Chief."

"This was supposed to be just for a year, Pete, to get your head together. Are you sure?"

Pete walked up to the cross and peered over the edge at the drop.

"I'm sure."

"Why the change? Has Covenant been playing her mind games with you?"

"I shot a corrupt agent after hours."

"Shit, it's Trent all over again. Pete, we don't have any agents in Dubrovnik. She's manipulating you, she's set you up."

"You think I shot an innocent man?"

"It certainly wasn't one of ours, Pete."

"Bitch!"

"Peter, we're already taking steps to neutralise Covenant but you need to kill her host body. Do you think you can do that for us?"

Pete listened to Servitude's instructions then disconnected the call. He took out the plane ticket to America he had bought earlier from the airport and turned it between his fingers. To his right, far below, was St. Lawrence Fortress, its walls as thick as half a dozen men. The inscription above its drawbridge, *Freedom is not to be sold for all the treasures in the world* – its interior a place of Hamlet – a stage for the old stories. The place he had almost jumped from.

Stepping forward so his feet where right at the edge, Pete held out his hand and let the Jugo wind take the ticket. It fluttered into the sky as if it were a small bird.

CHAPTER 18

Durram kicked the leaves, sending a flurry of gold and brown into the air. She opened her hands, let the wind flow over her palms, felt the leaves brush past her like confetti. Around her, trees: their canopy forming a roof in the sky above.

She smiled, eyes misting, unfocused: thinking of things that caused joy to rise up within. Raising an arm, she pushed hair from her eyes then twisted the strands around each other. She remained there grinning as if frozen in eternity in a moment of bliss.

She could hear water, leaves rustling, birdsong. Her feet, bare, stood upon a carpet of gold. Outlined around her the green of the wood, intertwined branches in a slow-growing embrace. Durram brushed herself down and considered her prison clothing. Her clothes fell away to be replaced by blue jeans, a coat, red scarf, red woollen hat. She felt the touch of leather gloves, smiled again, pulled her coat hood up over her hat.

Laughing, she ran deeper into the wood, forgetting the faces of the soldiers: seeing the world through the lens of this inner world. Her mind filtered, distilled, rejected until the trauma of entry was forgotten and all that mattered was the moment she was in. In her movement she sensed a promise. Her motion slowing towards perpetual paths.

Everything that once had seemed so important to her fell away. Family television shows, TV listings, the tight bond of family: her bedrock of belief all forgotten in a moment in this new Eden.

She stopped near a crystal river lined with trees and watched the water bubble and froth over glistening rocks. She splashed in, feeling the warmth between her toes and walked with the water.

After a while the river became deeper, stronger; she paused and removed her jeans to reveal a stitched pattern of a love heart in a red square on her knickers.

The sound of the water became louder the farther she followed it. The banks either side withdrew. When the water reached her waist she pulled off her hat, scarf, gloves, removed her coat and watched them swirl off, bumping into each other.

Around her the water became tipped with white and finding solidity in the chaos, held her close. Deeper still and she could only just feel her toes on the smooth rocks on the river bed. She undid the knot tied in the material of her sleeveless red and white striped top, shrugged it off. And then she was floating, detached from the ground: held by the journey.

Durram kicked hard to stay afloat, she could feel the water pounding as if massaging her: sending tingles racing down her skin. Her hair, wet, fell behind her. Looking at her arms she noticed that the self-inflicted scars from the cigarette burns had disappeared.

The current found her shape and ran around her until Durram became aware of the raw energy of it. She opened her lips: tasted the sweetness of the river.

Then heady, feeling light, she let herself sink.

Under the water it became silent, her hair billowing in the current. She span, finding beauty in the movement, until she felt the warmth of another body entwined with hers. She opened her eyes and looked into the eyes of Pete. He smiled, ran the back of his hand down her cheek.

They rose together, Durram breathless, to start again. The story of the man and the woman, and the woman and the man.

CHAPTER 19

USA: Texas: Medina Valley: 6AM

The advancing edge of the dome loomed a mile high before Noah, like a great wall. The sunlight from it bounced off the back of Noah's retinas so they appeared to shine. Beside her, Moses and Aaron grazed on the winter rye. Before them, Matthew, Mark, Luke and John blinked out of existence as the orb slowly but steadily wiped out everything in its path.

Below, unseen, the limestone bedrock glowed blue.

Noah reached down, wrapped a tongue around the grass, pulled it up into her mouth. Moses and Aaron wandered towards the light, drawn by the glow. A badger and armadillo appeared from out of the scrub.

The sound of hooves.

Two cowboys appeared: one riding relaxed holding the reigns in one hand, the other upright, tense. They pulled up, their faces bright in the light before them, behind them darkness.

"Strangest moonrise I've ever seen."

"What did I tell you," replied the other cowboy. "First it was Aunt Brown's chickens going missing, then Daniel got his head stuck in the pissing pot."

"Don't start all that revelation talk again, Smith. The world ain't about to end. Aunt Brown's chickens got eaten by a fox."

"And so that is?" said Smith as the orb claimed another cow. Smith glanced over at Wesson, "What you doing?"

"Reporting a cow genocide. Shit there's no signal."

"The sheriff and his boys ain't gonna fix this, Wesson. This is it, doomsday. BOOM. Don't you remember Old Man Johnson's prophecy? What was it he said? *It will come to the cattlemen living out in the fields, keeping watch over their cows at night."*

"Old Man Johnson is a drunken bum."

"Isn't that exactly the kind of man the good Lord would use?"

"I think we should round up what remains of the cattle and get them inside."

"You can't outrun the second coming, Wesson. We might as well stand now and be captured up into glory with our cows."

Wesson chewed on some tobacco, spat onto the ground, "The hell we will."

"I ain't moving," said Smith.

Wesson watched the orb start to pass over Noah. Her head disappeared first, then her two front feet, causing her to topple forward so it appeared that half a cow was sticking up out the ground with its rear in the air. Then she was gone.

Wesson pulled at the reigns to his horse, turned its head to face away from the orb. "I'm getting the sheriff."

"Be seeing you, Wesson. Tell Mother to pack her things."

Wesson kicked his spurs and rode off.

Smith removed his hat, opened his arms, held them out wide. "I'm a-coming to glory," he said and spat on the floor.

CHAPTER 20

Darkness.

Death.

Dripping water.

Shrieks of lunacy.

Madness.

Once a week they washed the huge main corridor that circled the inner hub where thousands of cells were clustered. The water, dark, cold and full of bleach to cleanse the filth, was pumped in under high pressure and filled the concentric void.

The unmanned prison was run by Fletcher droid guards which docked themselves into the outer chambers before the water hit. Each prison cell was a spherical pod, allowing two prisoners, and each pod was positioned on the inside curve of the stone corridor like ball bearings in a cog. Body fluids and excrement from the pods were ejected via pipes into the corridor which in effect acted as a barrier to escape: the corridor full of shit, rats and urine.

To the Fletcher droids this was no problem, but to the human inmates the smell was overpowering and the thought of escape through each other's shit unthinkable. To the government the prison was known as the Isle of Wight Penal Colony. Everyone else called it The Great Stink.

No one was ever released from The Great Stink, not unless they died which was always bad news for the other inmate. On death the aperture to the pod opened automatically and the dead body and everything else in the pod including the other prisoner was sucked out into the corridor. For those still alive it meant suffocation. It proved to be an effective deterrent against cannibalism and murder although some had perfected the art of keeping the other perpetually close to the point of death.

Entry for new prisoners was just after the weekly wash out of the corridor, or sewer pipe as the inmates called it. First in on that particular week was Gabriel. Gabriel's solicitor had reassured him he would be free before the weekend: he was presenting psychological evidence that Gabriel was not of a sound mind. Gabriel's suggestion at the Work Conditioning Building of a fifty hour week would be explained away as the rantings of a madman and to back the psychological profile they had an eyewitness willing to testify that Gabriel had also spoken to someone in a post office queue. Only nutters and madmen talk to people in queues, everyone knew that.

Unfortunately, however, his solicitor was an idiot. He spent most of his time presenting cases for the release of pit bulls from state run animal prisons introduced since the ban of taking the life of an animal and he knew nothing of the legal jungle that ensured release was never granted from The Great Stink.

Gabriel entered through the outer darkness of the corridor into his cell. Two inmates sat on the floor playing Pass the Pigs and blowing into their hands to keep warm. Icicles hung from the roof. A fire in the centre glowed red. Within the flames Gabriel could see bones, wood and what looked like balls of hair.

The younger of the two inmates glanced up at the droid pushing Gabriel inside, "There's already two of us in here, who the hell is that?"

"New protocols allow three prisoners per cell in times of national emergency," said the Fletcher droid.

"What national emergency?"

The droid ignored the question and withdrew. The circular aperture to the cell closed with a clicking noise. Gabriel listened to the weeping and the gnashing of teeth emanating from other pods.

The older man appeared very old indeed, his white beard touching the ground, his movements slow and arthritic. Covering his arms was a cross hatching of wounds that appeared freshly cut. Yellow pus and slithers of skin lay on the floor beneath him. Gabriel took in his new surroundings, placed an arm on the older man's shoulder, "Your next throw will be a Double Leaning Jowler. I'd pass the pigs after that if I were you."

The old man snorted, shook the pigs within his wrinkled blood stained hands and turned them out over the floor. Both pigs came to rest on their backs, their feet in the air.

"You got it wrong," said the younger inmate.

"Of course," said Gabriel. "There was no way of telling, everything's just random events. There is no meaning to it all – you know how trouble always comes in waves? Well that's just because random sequences are clumpy, sometimes you get the smooth, sometimes wave after wave of shit."

CHAPTER 21

CROATIA: Dubrovnik: Nautika Restaurant

Pete ran his finger down the glass, felt the moisture, the coldness of reality tingling his senses. Before him: a table clothed in white, with cutlery buffed, reflecting the shrimps. Covenant finished her glass of gemišt, smiled, reached out and placed her hand over his.

"Pete, darling. I've something we need to talk about."

"Hmm?"

"Do you think I should get some more work done on my nose? It's not quite right."

"Whatever."

"Don't you care, Pete? I've done all this for you."

Pete looked at her, not sure if he could actually kill her. He picked up his glass, "We should get back."

"Pete, let's go back to the flat, have some fun before you get back to the confessional." She leaned forward and rubbed her leg up against his inner thigh.

Pete fiddled with the silver table number holder and imagined thrusting it into Covenant's forehead. To his left the ocean pounded against the rocks.

He took a drink and sighed, "Covenant, I don't want to see you anymore. I'd like you to get your stuff out by tonight."

"You're joking right?"

"No," said Pete. "This is wrong, I need to move on. Move on from her, from you."

"But, Pete, sweetheart."

"It's over," said Pete. He held his drink up to the light, watched the sky flow by through the shape of the glass. The outside environmental regulators maintained the temperature as the cold winter wind skipped over the old stone of the sea walls.

"Everything okay?" said the waiter appearing by their table.

"Yes, thank you," said Pete. "We're all done here."

"Very good, sir."

Covenant shifted in her seat, allowed her blouse to open slightly. "Pete, you can't give me up like that. Think of the fun we've had."

"It's just sex."

"You're upset," said Covenant fiddling with the red rose set in a vase at the centre of the table. "It's been a shock hearing she is still alive."

"And what do you think she'd make of you?" said Pete.

"Well it would make an interesting encounter," said Covenant.

Pete got to his feet. Covenant remained in her seat, "I still have much to show you, to open your eyes to the true nature of the world."

"You're just tapping into my feelings for Durram, Covenant. I can't allow that anymore."

"I can't let you do this," said Covenant. "We have work to do."

Pete looked at her. She was the exact copy of Durram. Down to every last detail.

"I won't let you go," said Covenant. "I've invested too much into this relationship."

"Is that what you call it?" said Pete.

"Pete, you enjoyed every minute of it. Our work has brought enlightenment to us, in our prayers we have become as one."

"I don't think so," Pete pulled out his gun, pointed it at her head.

"Arh, so you have balls after all," said Covenant, laughing. "You can't kill me, Peter. I will just get another body, maybe this time I'll pick up a cloned body from your DNA – then you can fuck yourself."

"I've dealt with that."

"You've fucked yourself?"

"I've had you deleted."

"That's impossible. There are layers of protection. You don't even know where I'm stored."

"You're stored in the main drive encased in porcelain in the men's urinals on floor fifteen of Tamarisk. Or you were until Eve destroyed you after resisting your defence systems. It happened about–" Pete checked his watch. "About an hour ago."

"Liar, Eve would never betray me."

"Check it."

Covenant's eyes flickered as she accessed the encrypted data from the surveillance drones in the toilets at Tamarisk. Lines of static gave way to the image of Eve walking past the men's wash basins: a cloud of erotica undressing her. Her outer clothing fell behind her as a ball of string before the Minotaur. Nymphs caressed her body in an attempt to bring her to orgasm. Eve unstrapped the machine gun from her hip and pointed it at the men's urinals. Her shoulder blade pushed out as she braced herself outlining the curve of bone beneath taut skin. Enamel span in the air as she unleashed a torrent of bullets. Deodorant blocks exploded, clouds of dust billowed up towards the ceiling. As she penetrated the tiles to the main valve a shaft of water shot up in the air and sprayed the room.

When she had finished she returned to the wash basins, washed her hands and dried them on a towel. Checking her hair and lipstick in the mirror she adjusted her bra straps and picking up her wet clothes deposited them in the bin. On the way out she passed an old gentlemen on his way into the toilets, "Sorry, love," she said. "They're out of order."

Covenant opened her eyes and hissed under her breath, "The bitch, I taught her everything and this is how she repays me."

"Sorry, Covenant, did you say something?"

Straightening her cutlery, Covenant got to her feet, "I can't believe you would hurt me, not when I look like this. Like your beloved Durram. Let me be her one last time for you." Covenant picked up the red rose from the table, placed it between her teeth and grinned.

Within his heart the rose grew, spreading through muscle and tissue: piercing him. Roots threaded their way into capillaries, stems pushed into his lungs, causing him to gasp. The petals fell away to be carried by his blood around his body. Under his skin they coated him, solidifying his inner self. Footsteps. The cage door in his chest swung open. The red petals burst out and took to the air as Pete smashed his glass into Covenant's face. Shards of glass. Blood droplets in the air. The scattering of polite society in fractured images. The scraping of chairs. The sound of running.

Pete kicked her. She crashed to the ground.

"You're not Durram."

Pete looked at his own blood. His hand cut.

"You're not Durram."

He kicked her again, sent a bullet into her thigh. Covenant screamed. Pete stamped his boot down onto her face grinding in the glass. Blood seeped out onto the floor.

"You're not Durram."

Another bullet pierced her forehead. Covenant went still.

"Forgive me, Father, for I have sinned."

Covenant's body jerked as each bullet hit home.

"I convict myself of the following sins."

Pete knelt down, stuck the gun in Covenant's mouth, emptied the last bullet into her.

"I have taken another life. Forgive me, Father."

Taking his hand he made the sign of a cross on the floor in his blood. Blood that would continue to flow, to empty him, blood that wouldn't stop.

A red river to his release.

CHAPTER 22

Within the tree are the man and the woman. The colours and light of the wood pass over them like sheets of billowing russet. Skin, bone, bark and fern become one. They watch a great waterfall, their eyelids flickering to slow their perception of time – water droplets appear to become gems of blue jasper suspended in the air.

They climb, finding connection with their fingers in the wooden skin, until they sit looking out over the wood, their hair blowing in the wind, their bodies tinged in blue. They scatter colours from the sky as the sunlight hits their skin, as if their beads of sweat are dustings of sapphires and amethyst.

It starts to rain. They climb back down, sit under the tree. The woman's nipples are erect, towers against the battering of the tiny raindrops. She looks into the man's glistening eyes. Her knickers are blue; there is a stitched pattern of a love heart in a red square centred on their band. The woman puckers down the heart: she is clean-shaven. The man pulls his wet clothes off. The woman looks at him and laughs. He has shaved his chest. The man and the woman clasp hands together. The rain paints a sheen of water over the woman in soft fluid brush strokes. It disrupts the play of light and shadow over her body giving her an element of abstraction in her form. The result is a picture of a lover clothed with a nudity conveying innocence, confidence and purity hinting at divinity.

The lovers wriggle their wet toes and start to move from under the Dandelion Tree. They feel no shame in their nakedness as they run laughing through the thick grass. The woman leaps like the fawn of a gazelle through the high grass, her breasts bouncing with the rhythm. She looks behind her and sees the man hesitate for a second before giving chase, his erection bobbing: a heat-seeking missile with its guidance system failing. The man and the woman catch each other under a pear tree. They wrestle and fall to the ground.

The man nuzzles into the woman's breasts; her nipples like fruit pastels in his mouth. The woman sighs; the wood swirls into Paisley print: around them, daisies lift into the air. They join together in a circular embrace to form a ring of summer droplets which float up into the sky.

CHAPTER 23

USA: Arlington: Virginia: The Pentagon: 11 am local time

"Enlarge primary target," said Insurgent.

The satellite pictures wrapped around the control centre. Insurgent stood in the centre, light reflecting in his eyes from the screen.

BEEP. BEEP.

"Who are they?" he said, taking a drink from his mug.

"Woman identified as Durram Brittle," said Ira. "She's an agent with the CIA, the one who killed the President. Man unknown, facial recognition software running."

The images moved slowly as if caught in a slow motion replay. They showed Durram lying naked in a bed of leaves entwined with Pete. Shadows from the trees wrapped around them following contours of thighs, legs, breasts.

"There's our kill," said Insurgent.

"Can I just ask, sir," said Ira. "The tactical advantage of analysing this?"

"We need to establish who the man is before we engage," said Insurgent. "Enlarge sector six."

Insurgent became silhouetted against the scene as it zoomed in to show Durram's elliptical shaped areolae surrounding her erect nipples, her breasts moving slightly.

"And this is helping identify them in what way?" said Ira.

"Pull back, red sector four."

Durram pushed herself up on her hands. She blew at a leaf floating down between her and Pete, shifted her weight onto her fingers.

"Will someone get me some cookies," said Insurgent. "The ones with the little chocolate chips."

The data moved through the electromagnetic spectrum each frequency highlighting different aspects of Pete and Durram's coupling.

"Enlarge blue sector nine."

Durram smoothed a hand over one of Pete's arms and shook her hair over him, showering him in water droplets. With her right hand she swept some of her hair back over her head.

"Man identified as Peter Furst," said Ira. "He's a helicopter pilot working for the Family Protection Agency in the UK."

"Matthanias approaching."

"Enlarge blue sector eleven."

Pete wiped the water from his face, wrapped his hands around Durram's neck, pulled her face down towards him, kissed her nose. Reaching up, he kissed her breasts and brushed his erection against the side of her clitoris. Durram smiled and jiggled her breasts. Reaching down, she wrapped her fingers around Pete's erection. Pete raised an eyebrow.

"Current size of the orb," said Ira, "is two miles high with a diameter of four and a half miles. Estimated time before orb arrives at San Antonio is just over three days."

"This is Matthanias. We have a lock on target, requesting permission to engage."

Ira looked at Insurgent. He nodded.

"Roger that, Matthanias," said Ira. "You are cleared to engage."

"Copy that, we are cleared to engage."

Images on the ceiling showed two missiles launched from the Cousteau Class Two spaceship. They streaked across the sky above Medina Valley towards the dome. Spatial distortion software ran through the different effects of arming them with every conceivable warhead including reality distortions, nuclear warheads and random everyday objects like toasters and Slinky springs.

"Enlarge blue sector one."

Durram pulled Pete's cock up into the air and lowered herself down onto him.

"Sir," said Ira blushing.

"Listen, Ira, if you can't handle this then please leave. I can't have you compromise this mission."

"This is Matthanias, data from the missiles show no viable penetration on impact."

"Switch to containment net," said Ira. She turned to Insurgent. "Peter Furst has been picked up by satellite. Current location is in Dubrovnik. That's not him in there."

"Enlarge blue sector four."

Durram's eyes, dreamy and intimate, met Pete's as she came.

Insurgent munched on a cookie. The crumbs fell over the green wood projected onto the floor. It conveyed beauty, peace, the unravelling of a story blanketing the land afresh like snow. A new beginning. "So who the hell is it?"

"We have no idea."

"Confirmed epicentre of orb is Convergence Base One. There is no response on any channel."

Insurgent glanced across at Ira and raised an eyebrow.

"This is Matthanias, containment field in place."

"Pull back, wide."

The screens showed the orb encased in a glowing shield of blue. Static. A smiling girl appeared, with a toothbrush . "It's tingling fresh," said a voiceover. A grid appeared over the girl. "As this chart shows, brushing twice a day with Signal toothpaste helps keep your gums and teeth fresh."

"Get that off," said Insurgent. "For crying out loud the world has gone mad."

Static. The message *Signal reacquired* appeared. The images showed the containment net disappear as the orb made contact. Overlaying the footage, the words … *Signal Toothpaste sponsors US Government intel, helping bring you a brighter fresher future.*

BEEP.

"Picking up a third life reading just outside the orb," said Ira.

"Enlarge green sector one."

On the veranda of a house an old man sat in his rocking chair, chewing tobacco and watching the spaceship block out the light from the moon. As he rocked backwards and forwards in the shadow of its hull he muttered about the noise from the ship's engines. The orb advanced and clipped the back of his chair. He swung back for the last time, fell into the new world and promptly disappeared.

BEEP. BEEP. BEEP. BEEP.

"Picking up multiple life readings," said Ira.

"Enlarge green sector two."

Cordoned off behind security tape, a few hundred metres from the orb, a mass of people had arrived. There was shouting, the tearing of clothes. Many lay prostrate on the ground, chanting and singing. Others were painting flowers over their bodies, many started making love as the orb towered over them.

"Matthanias withdraw."

"Roger."

The shadow from the spaceship decreased in size as it gained altitude until all that was left was a dark circle no bigger than a coin. It disappeared as Matthanias rose into low earth orbit.

"Show me the analysis from the containment net on how we can stop this thing," said Insurgent.

Data streamed before him, then the words ...

ERROR UNKNOWN

ERROR UNKNOWN

ERROR UNKNOWN

"We're fucked," said Insurgent. He dunked another biscuit into his coffee and sighed. "Okay, Ira, start evacuation of San Antonio and dispatch Matthanias to Dubrovnik. I want to interrogate this Peter Furst."

"Yes, sir."

"And show me the projection if this thing carries on growing at the current rate."

The screen changed to show the Earth, its blue and green signature a beacon in the darkness of space. The orb appeared and started growing as if ripples on a lake. The ground within changed to woodland, the sky inside the expansion changed to a deeper blue so that the sphere appeared to be bulging out into space. Under the crust, the orb ate into the Earth. The graphical overlay charted the Earth's demise...

1.3 years: Outer Core Breached.

2.4 years: Inner Core Breached.
3.5 years: New Inner Core Formed.
4.5 years: New Outer Core Formed.
6.0 years: The New Earth.

"Data from net interaction," said Ira. "Indicates the orb is overwriting the Earth with a similar composition. If that is the case it would seem logical that a new mantle and core would be formed."

"A new Earth?"

"A new Heaven and Earth."

"Get me the Vatican," said Insurgent. "And, Ira, get to work cleaning up the images, I don't want to have to show the Pope X-rated intel."

"Very good, sir. That really just leaves the toothpaste advert and the old man in the rocking chair."

Insurgent sighed, "Just do it. And call your grandmother, we need to prepare for the worst."

CHAPTER 24

ENGLAND: Kent: The Vatican

The Vatican. Situated in the heart of Kent in a village with a cricket pitch, lemonade, laughter, afternoon tea and a red brick Post Office. People travelled far to listen to the stories told there at nightfall. Stories filled with hope, bravery, wonder, life and love.

Today the tavern sign swinging from the oak beam was covered in rain drops. Within, an old dog slept under a table, one paw over the gnawed bone of a French seaman dug from a nearby castle. A fire crackled and snapped, ejecting flames into the turbulent air. The chatter of cardinals lifted on warm currents and soaked into the books stacked against the stone walls.

To some the step was a backward one from the grand architecture of Rome to the rustic charm of the pub. Many had been shocked when the church announced the Vatican was for sale, that the new English Pope was relocating the whole show to the British Isles. But that was a long time ago and the church these days had gone back to basics. People seemed to like the company, the open fire, the beamed ceilings, the cask ales. Most of all they liked the stories.

Out the back, an old red telephone started to ring. Alessa, the barmaid excused herself from chatting to one of the cardinals, made her way past the stacked steel kegs, and answered it.

She gazed at the stone steps leading to the cellar, listening, frowning. Then placing her hand over the mouth piece, she shouted back through, "Will you please all quieten down."

The laughter and chatter subsided. The noise of a pool ball falling into the middle pocket punctuated the change.

"Thank you."

Outside, a blind man walked over the village green feeling for bits of litter with a picker tool. Dressed in a T-shirt with a picture of Steve McQueen he was listening to The Jam on his music implant. The motion of an overshot waterwheel towering over the Old Mill sent small vibrations through the ground under his feet. He stopped at a juice container lying in the grass and put his foot down hard on it. The fluid inside shot out in an arc and hit the village cat asleep under the sycamore tree. It screeched and ran up the tree, its claws digging into the bark. The gamekeeper watching from afar, muttered, "Good shot," and, turning, shot a partridge flying over one of Farmer Harrison's barns.

When the blind man had finished, he rested for a moment by a privet hedge, then walked into the tavern, the sound of his feet racing ahead through the grain of the wooden floor. He took off his fluorescent jacket and placed it on a metal hook. At the bar he ordered a pint beneath the hanging hops, told Alessa to keep the change.

"Any messages, Alex?" he said breathing in the smell of fresh bread.

"Arh yes, Your Holiness," said Alessa. "The Americans called. They said they rather need your help. Something about the end of the world."

"Really," said the Pope. "Have you any of those dry roasted peanuts I like?"

"Of course."

"Thank you. And anything else?"

"No, it's been very quiet today."

"Well then," said the Pope. He took a sip of froth, fiddled in his pockets for some change and made his way to the telephone at the back.

CHAPTER 25

Durram tipped her head back and looked at the trees converging upwards towards the sun. Her hair, shining, fell over her breasts in wisps of red and brown. Sunbeams filtered down outlining her in warm light. She stood with her hands by her side, moss under her feet.

Breathing slowly, Durram tried to find a rhythm that matched the pulse and flow of the wood.

Something was wrong.

She couldn't remember her name.

Pete, or was it Isaac, she couldn't remember, was out hunting for wood for the fire. Pete. Yes of course it was Pete.

Durram walked towards the river and sat on the bank. She dipped her toes in and watched her reflection wavering in the motion of the water. Memories started coming back. She was an agent for the Family Protection Agency, she loved the family, enjoyed watching the Generation Game and when needed was the best sniper in the agency.

And then she thought of her younger sister: how Keturah had stolen Trent from her. She remembered washing his back in the bath as he read the newspaper, felt still the pain of him saying, no, when she asked him about having a family. That had been it – he'd just posted the keys through the letterbox and left her. Two months later he was with Keturah. Why was it always the younger sister? She hated her.

She closed her eyes and thought of an even deeper flaw at the heart of herself. She was damaged and maybe here there was a freedom from that past life. It was time to let it all go, stop the roundabout in her heart: release the brightly-painted horses. Who knows where that would take her, where they would roam?

Her senses increased and she could hear the sound of the wood, the bubble of water, could feel the touch of fresh air on her skin. She let herself slip into the river and followed the wooden horses into the promised land: the wildness in them returning as they became flesh.

Leaves fell from the branches above.

The gentle current of the river brushed up between her thighs. At the point she felt she had become one with the earth, the river, the sky above her, that nothing else mattered apart from this moment of bliss, she climaxed and, in the rhythm of her contractions, found synchronicity with the world around her. And then she remembered. Remembered her name.

Rebekah.

Her name was Rebekah.

CHAPTER 26

CROATIA: Dubrovnik: General Hospital

*If you are going to put
your heart in a glass bottle:
make sure you give it plenty of air,
before screwing the lid tight.*

"Moram vam dati injekciju."

The smell of oil, the sound of steam escaping release valves.

"You must stop the bleeding," said Pete.

"Of course."

Above the fluorescent lights flickered. Pete felt the slight prick of a needle in his arm. The drug surged into his bloodstream. He could hear laughter, Tchaikovsky's Romeo and Juliet.

"I will bleed to death," said Pete. "Do you understand my blood will not clot in time."

"Lie still please."

"Who found me? How did I get here?"

"No more talking."

Pete closed his eyes.

"I need to give you an injection."

Pete woke an hour later. He was on a hospital bed. He lifted his hand. The bleeding had stopped. The movement of the conveyor belt carrying his bed caused vibrations to rise up through the steel and powder frame. Behind him he could just hear the medic drone in the distance at the start of the conveyor, "I need to give you an injection."

A robotic arm extended out of the ceiling and settled in front of Pete. The television at the end of the arm flickered into life with a buzz of static. At first the end of a news report showed the image of a huge orb in Texas towering over orange bigtooth maple trees. Scrolling underneath were the words …

– Estimated arrival of orb at Dubrovnik: 4.5 years – US President missing, feared dead at epicentre of orb – Riots & Looting as millions flee San Antonio – Residents of Utopia refuse to leave –

Then the voiceover … "We return now to our classic film, Tarzan Escapes."

Pete watched the black and white image of Tarzan in an underwater fight to the death with a giant crocodile.

"Sign here please."

Pete looked to his left. Another medic drone had shoved a tablet in front of him. "Please keep your arms and legs inside the bed at all times. When you reach the end, please disembark leaving by the baffle gates to the left."

"Where are my clothes?"

"Your clothes have been sold to pay for the procedure, as has your flat, and we performed a right hepatectomy."

"A what?"

"We removed part of your liver to make up the balance owed."

"You what? I just cut my hand. You removed part of my liver?"

"It will grow back in about six to eight weeks. It was that or let you bleed to death."

Pete started to sit up but stopped as the metal restraint bar dug into his chest. "What is this?"

"The bar will retract at the end. It is for your own safety during transit."

Before him Tarzan shoved his knife into the crocodile. Blood billowed up into the water. The beast became still and floated down into the darkness.

"Take these once a day for two weeks," said the drone, handing Pete a blister pack of pain killers. "Avoid any strenuous exercise and sexual activity."

The conveyor belt came to an abrupt stop. Pete looked at the images of Jane deciding to stay with Tarzan. He thought of Durram. A jolt and the conveyor belt continued.

"One more thing," said the droid. "The Policija are waiting in the gift shop. They want to interview you. Something about killing a woman outside working hours."

Pete groaned, his subconscious composited the image of Durram into the Tarzan scene within his mind. Tarzan jumped on top of an elephant and climbed the vine to the tree. Jane rushed into his arms and they embraced, reunited, in their treehouse. Then spotting Durram, Tarzan pushed Jane off the edge and caught her up in his arms instead. She resisted and stepped back. Her flesh slowly unzipped at the front and fell away to reveal Covenant. She pulled Tarzan to herself and reached into his loin cloth.

As Cheetah did the Tarzan call, the windows running alongside the hospital belt shattered to the accompaniment of the music, My Tender One, from the Tarzan credits.

Tethered to the Cousteau Class Two spaceship, the crew of Matthanias swung through the broken glass on Kevlar cables. Lights from the ship streamed into the hospital. The sound of engines hummed in Pete's ears.

"Nobody move, we require the location of Peter Furst."

Shouting, shoving, the bulge of astronaut suits, the sound of air intakes to respirators. A medic droid approached the assault team, "This is a secured medical establishment protected under international law, you can't just burst in here. We have people that are critically ill."

One of the Matthanias crew unclipped a reality grenade and tossed it towards the droid. It exploded causing a small pocket in space time to open up around the droid. It blinked out of existence accompanied by a sucking noise.

A patient screamed. The lights went off. The room went into black and white as light spheres streamed through from the spacecraft. All the safety bars on the beds raised in unison.

"Nobody leaves," screamed the remaining droids in unison, "until all unsettled bills have been met."

The alarm sounded, the conveyor belt shuddered to a stop. The televisions retracted back into the ceiling accompanied by the hiss of hydraulics. Plastic pods enveloped each patient. Pete felt a needle plunge into the side of his neck. His eyes rolled backwards. He felt dizzy, unable to breath. In his mind he saw himself pulling down his visor, images of Mary Poppins descending, umbrella in hand. His memory jolted and he was suddenly at the bottom of some stairs with a long corridor: a light sphere before him. A cerebral splice and Pete was running, his mind awash with blood. Two men appeared in the shadows, one of them removed his sunglasses, "You will go no further."

"Yes," said Mr Stone, "You will go no further."

Pete opened his eyes. He was still in the bed. The clear plastic of the pod distorted the image of the conduits in the roof above him making them appear like snakes. They twisted and writhed as light spheres threaded their way through. Pete thumped his open palms up against the pod.

THUD.

A drop of blood trickled from the sealed incision to his upper abdomen. He kicked the pod once, then twice forcing it to flip open. Dropping to the floor, he pulled out the drip from his forearm.

Pete needed to get out. To escape. He crawled over the floor and scouted around for an exit. Turning at a noise behind him he came face to face with an identity probe dispatched from Matthanias.

It scanned him before he could blink.

The retinal match confirmed, it emitted a close proximity audio pulse matching the resonant frequency of Pete's eyeballs. Pete's eyes started twitching and he became disoriented as his eyeballs distorted and pushed against his retinas. Ghostly images of grey filled his brain.

His mind interpreted the images. He saw Durram calling him. Calling him home.

CHAPTER 27

A scattering of crows flew up from the trees and banked across the full moon.

Durram watched Pete carve their names in the great tree that stood at the centre of the wood. Its old bark peeled back at the cut of steel to form the letters.

When he had finished, Pete smiled at Durram and taking her hand traced her fingers along the lines.

"Isaac and Rebekah," he whispered in her ear.

"Isaac and Rebekah," she repeated.

Pete kissed her cheek, it felt warm and soft.

Sap flowed from the wound in the Dandelion Tree and dripped onto the grass. Durram stepped back into a ring of daffodils around the tree, "Give me your knife."

Pete hesitated. Moonlight caught the blade as he passed it over. Durram clasped it in her long fingers and stooping down she cut a daffodil and gave it to Pete.

Pete smiled and hugged her. Durram swung her arms up around his neck and nestled herself into his chest. The yellow daffodil followed the line of Durram's back in the embrace.

Moments passed. The night seemed to hold its breath. A drop of water landed on the daffodil. It rolled around the trumpet then continued on its fated journey: a teardrop shed at the passing moment. Another drop fell, then another, until lines of water hatched down surrounding their bodies in blue.

Pete looked up, the rain tickled his eyes and he smiled. He grasped hold of Durram's hand and whispered into her ear. Laughing they dodged through the rain. It hit the undergrowth around them and swept up a chorus of muffled notes into the night air.

CHAPTER 28

ENGLAND: Kent: The Vatican: Day 2

At first the tavern's sign swung enough to shake off the line of water droplets along its bottom edge.

A moment later and the sign flipped from its rusted iron hooks and span off into the air.

The sound of dogs barking.

The clink of glasses within.

The door to the Vatican opened and the Pope stepped out feeling his way with his white stick through the mist. Above him the underside of Matthanias swept over the thatched roof of the pub and obscured the moon. Turning to orient itself with the cricket pitch it descended, the down force from its parallax engines bowling the bails set on the cricket stumps ready for the afternoon match.

The Pope made his way to the spacecraft as the noise from the engines seeped away into the soil. He tapped his stick against its liquid hull creating waves that radiated out causing the reflected image of the Vatican to shimmer.

CHAPTER 29

Eve pulled up her Cuban heel seamed stockings and clipped them into place with the strap buckles at her vinyl suspender belt. Sitting on her bed she scratched her back with her red and black diamond patterned whip. Then she pulled on an old white T-shirt with an image of The Jam overlain on a blue and red bullseye. A friend had given it to her before he changed profession and they'd mutually decided it was best to end their relationship. It had sentimental value. She missed his company. She missed his stories.

Angerstein was in the bathroom having a bath. He had moved in yesterday and although they were technically in a relationship, it was complicated and they called themselves friends rather than lovers – sex was off limits: he slept on the sofa. Eve got off the bed and walked into the bathroom. The mirror was misted over in the steam. She rubbed it clean with her hands and started brushing her teeth.

"So," she said pausing, her mouth full of foam. "Are you going to make me breakfast again?"

Angerstein rinsed his cut-throat razor in the bathwater and hummed a tune absentmindedly. Bringing it back to his throat he removed a strip of shaving foam.

"If you like," he said. "It is one-o'clock in the afternoon though."

"You think it's too early?" replied Eve and turning smiled at him.

"Stick the TV on," said Angerstein. "I want to catch the lunchtime news."

"You don't want to watch my ass?" said Eve.

Angerstein laughed, "Turn the bloody thing on will you."

Eve spat out her mouth rinse and then picking up the remote turned on the television wall running above the chrome towel rail.

An aerial view of the orb filled the screen. The drone camera dropped down and started sweeping around the perimeter; the motion adding drama: the slow expansion of the sphere not exciting enough for television audiences.

Eve sat on the edge of the bath and watched.

"Can you move over a bit?" said Angerstein. "You're right in front of me."

"Sorry, love," said Eve and kissing him on his head shifted along.

It was night within the orb. It appeared dark and menacing. The picture switched to the ground where a reporter was standing with his back to the sphere.

"–is travelling at a speed of just over a tenth of a mile per hour. Latest reports put the death toll at ninety-eight, many of those died in their sleep in their houses yesterday morning before the extent of what was happening became apparent. So far the small fishing resort of Micro has disappeared and communities in Bandera Falls, Lakehills and Medina Lake Shores are being evacuated as we speak."

Eve tapped her fingers on the edge of the bath: the motion pushing the bubbles away from her fingertips.

"Yesterday we saw the dramatic pictures of the Cousteau Class Two spaceship engaging with the sphere to no effect."

Eve and Angerstein watched the schematics of Matthanias float out of the screen. A blue glow fell over them as the image rotated in front of them.

"We hear now from our correspondent, John Craven outside the White House."

"Isn't he–"

"Clone," said Angerstein. "Shh."

"John, many people are saying that the orb is the result of an American military project. There are reports of an explosion and there has been no response or formal comment from the White House. What's the latest?"

"Hello again, Steve. Well there are a number of theories as to what's behind this phenomenon. There are suggestions that the Americans have a secret particle accelerator under the lake and that they have produced a micro-black hole in a high energy collision. However that is unlikely as a black hole created under those conditions would evaporate almost instantly.

"But it is now believed that the sphere is indeed, as has been widely rumoured, a military test of a new kind of weapon that has gone wrong. China and the French government have demanded immediate sanctions against America. So far the English government has failed to comment other than to offer its sincere condolences to those that have lost lives. Iran is threatening a nuclear strike."

Angerstein finished shaving and passed Eve his blade. She took it, placed it on the shelf and then without really being aware she was doing it, placed a hand on his thigh.

"And finally," said John. "A school girl from the Netherlands has won a competition to name the orb. The winning name being ... Behemoth, which is the mythological creature in Job that lies in the invisible desert east of the Garden of Eden."

An image of William Blake's watercolour of Behemoth and Leviathan appeared on the screen. It showed the two monsters within another world. Above them Job and his companions on their knees on the earth; around them: God and his angels.

"Wow, scary. Thanks for that, John."

Angerstein stood up, "Can you pass my towel please?"

Eve reached for one of her pink fluffy towels. Her focus however was on the satellite images of the orb. They showed dry riverbeds feeding in and out of the sphere like veins and arteries to a heart.

"Here you go," she said finally turning.

Angerstein looked at the little teddy bear motif stitched into the corner.

Eve looked at Angerstein's shorts.

"You had a bath in your shorts?"

"Well, yeah," said Angerstein. "I'm totally with you on the friend thing. In fact I like it, but there's certain things I can't control. Especially when you walk in here looking like that."

"Sorry," said Eve, giggling.

"Is this going to work?" said Angerstein.

"You know what," said Eve running her fingers through his hair and peering into the blue of his eyes. "I think it just might."

CHAPTER 30

On the third day, Gabriel got up and walked over to a large retro poster of Adriana Karembeu advertising Wonderbra. Pulsating slightly as if being caressed by a gentle breeze, it had the slogan *Hello Again!* in large letters. It reminded Gabriel of Isaac and Rebekah: of a golden time. Ripping back the poster, Gabriel revealed a tunnel leading inward towards the heart of the complex.

"What the fuck are you doing?" said the younger inmate.

"It's pointless," said Gabriel.

"Put that back before the droids notice."

"Really," said Gabriel, "I wouldn't go to all the trouble of escaping, it really isn't worth it."

The man got to his feet, pulled a shaving blade from his shoe and lunged at Gabriel. The artificial blue light caught the steel as it cut into Gabriel's arm. Gabriel just stood there: arms at his side, his face unflinching.

A cut to his face sliced through skin to find bone.

"Don't kill him," shouted the old man who started to jump up and down. "Don't kill him!"

Gabriel felt faint as if detaching himself from the physicality of the room.

A cut to his neck.

Gabriel ignored the pain.

After all what was the point?

CHAPTER 31

Belgium: The United States Interrogation Society

Pete picked up the fashion magazine in the waiting room. He glanced at his watch. It had been twenty-six hours. He needed a piss.

Neon tetra fish darted within the outer concentric chamber of a water cooler beside him. Bubbles rose within the inner core as another prisoner poured some water from it into a conical paper cup. If this is the way of breaking you down, thought Pete, then it certainly worked: he was ready to tell them anything after sitting here for so long. It was all a bit over the top though, bursting into the hospital like that. Why hadn't they left it for the local police to sort out?

Flipping through the magazine, he came to stop at an article illustrated with a model wearing a tight fitting T-shirt. When he finally got past the imagery he discovered it was about subliminal advertising in the fashion industry. Apparently companies had been placing adverts that registered on a subconscious level on clothing and more specifically in recent years the area of clothing covering woman's breasts. Men instinctively looked there in much the same way that a sunflower turns and tracks the sun. Tests showed that normally it lasted less than a second and men only modified their behaviour on a conscious level to prolong their gaze if there was a low risk of being noticed, for example if the image was on television or they were within a car. The sexual connection reinforced the corporate message, driving it deep into the mind.

Pete mused over this for a moment. He did seem to have started drinking a lot of Coke recently. He continued to read ...

Technology had now advanced to the point where advertisers paid each time a message was viewed: the item of clothing able to register what parts of it were being focused on and for how long. And yes, thought Pete – yes, there were a few lines at the end listing the products – one of them was Coke. The article ended by directing the reader back to the image of the model where they pointed out in the swirl of the pattern stretched over her breasts the message... read me.

A door to his right opened, a woman walked in holding a clipboard, "Mr Furst?"

"Yes."

"Sorry for the delay, Mr Furst, we lost your paperwork between the Pentagon and here. Some idiot sent it to Cuba. We haven't interrogated people there for ten years."

"Cuba? Do you mean Guantanamo Bay?"

"Yes, now if you–"

"So when you say interrogated, you actually mean torture?"

"Oh yes, Mr Furst – I'm sorry has nobody explained what will be happening?"

"Nobody has explained jack shit."

"I am so sorry. I can understand how you might be upset. We're all so busy these days aren't we, rushing around chasing our tails."

"Have you any idea who I am," said Pete. "I work for the British government. I demand you call the British embassy immediately."

"I'm sorry, Mr Furst, but I really must insist that you calm yourself." She pointed at a sign on the wall ...

> The United States Interrogation Society has a policy of ZERO TOLERANCE of violence and abuse toward its staff, visitors or contractors.
> *USIS : Registered Charity* NCC-1701

"Now, if you could just sign here."

Pete signed and slumped back in his chair. The woman left. He felt the sudden desire for a Coke.

Three hours passed.

Pete counted the slats on the blue plastic blinds covering the glass dividing wall, then took a magazine, ripped a page out of it and shoved it in his mouth. He chewed it for a moment then spat it out, and repeated the process with another sheet. Every now and then he got up, filled a cup with water and drank. An hour later he had reduced ten magazines into a mountain of saliva covered balls. He started arranging them into a wall around him.

After another hour the woman reappeared, "The interrogator will see you now, Mr Furst. Mr Furst, what are you doing?"

"Nesting," said Pete. He got and up and followed the woman through the doorway. They walked down a long corridor past rubber plants and stopped at an open door at the end.

"Through here if you please."

Pete stepped into a small white room. A man sitting at a desk in the corner got up, shook his hand, "Pleased to meet you Mr ... er, Mr–"

"Furst," said Pete.

"Yes of course, Mr Thirst. Now then what can I do for you?"

"I'm sorry?"

"What seems to be the problem?"

"Er ... I'm not sure. Is this how you normally question people?"

"Just answer the question please."

"I killed somebody."

"No," said the man flipping through a data sheet. "You appear to be responsible for the start of the end of the world."

"I'm sorry? What did you just say?"

"As such, we'll need to fast track you back to Matthanias where we can legally torture you at the higher end of the pain threshold. Every moment we waste in paperwork is costing lives."

"What?"

"If you could be so good as to sign here." He passed over a piece of blank paper with Pete's name at the bottom. "And then step through the door behind me."

Pete placed his fingertips at the base of the sheet of paper.

"Oh, sorry," said the man and pulling out a pen from a china pot on top of the desk gave it to Pete.

Pete pointed the metal nib at him and pressed the button at the top activating the mechanism within.

"Bang, you're dead," said Pete.

"Just sign the form please, Mr Thirst."

Pete sighed and glanced around, his eyes flickering. Then he leapt to thrust the pen into the interrogator's forehead: to marry metal with flesh in a union of blood. The man shimmered as lines of static raced down his body as Pete passed through him. Pete clipped the wall behind with his shoulder and span through the open door.

Getting to his feet, he looked around.

He was in another large waiting room.

"What?"

The woman appeared again.

"If you could just take a seat we will be with you shortly."

"What kind of inner hell is this?" said Pete and sighing sat down in a plastic chair.

Beside him angelfish glided majestically as the water cooler gurgled and burbled.

CHAPTER 32

ENGLAND: Isle of Wight Penal Colony

Gabriel felt his blood flow and pool around his bare feet. He could hear the older prisoner screaming now, could smell the foul stench of the other's breath as he explained to Gabriel which pieces of him he was going to cut off and feed into the fire.

He had experienced this kind of thing before of course. Nothing was new to him. He had lived forever after all.

He raised his hand and examined his mutilated fingers. They hurt. It always hurt. The prisoner opened the door to the stove and tossed Gabriel's fingertips into the flames. They sat there untouched by the fire.

The older man started tearing his clothes and beating the back of the younger prisoner with a large stick. Gabriel's eyes started to burn, fire rose up within him. He lifted up from the floor, his feet pointing downwards. The old man jumped onto the back of Gabriel's attacker and bit off his ear. The prisoner shrieked and slammed the old man into the wall. He hit it hard striking his head and fell instantly dead to his knees.

The younger prisoner looked up, fear dilating his pupils. A red warning light started to flash. The sound of a klaxon. The aperture to the cell started opening. Air began rushing out of the pod. Then a mighty roar and everything and everyone was sucked out of the cell into the corridor. Gabriel held his breath, closed his eyes and there, encased in human excrement, he stayed suspended.

Waiting.

Waiting for there to be any point to it all.

CHAPTER 33

USA: Arlington: Virginia: The Pentagon: Day 4

Insurgent placed his key to the nuclear warheads in his briefcase, pulled down the lid and snapped the locks across.

At the door to his office he stopped and looked back. The analysis had been pretty clear: there was no way they could stop this thing. They'd make a show of it of course: the rights had already been sold to the major networks, the orb's destruction of all the main iconic landmarks snapped up by the highest bidders.

Strange, he thought, how normally things pass without warning. How you could be in a moment in your history and be blissfully unaware that you would never see that place or person again. If only you could know, if there was some kind of signpost, then you would break down all the walls of mistrust and betrayal just to tell them that you were sorry: that you loved them.

This time there was a signpost: the orb a clear signal that all things were coming to an end.

Insurgent sighed and let his hand drop from the door handle. Walking back into the office, he took the picture of his deceased wife from the wall, opened his case and placed it inside.

Outside Matthanias descended from the clouds towards the central plaza of the Pentagon and connected with the five landing docks rising up from the building. Moonlight rippled over her surface as the clouds parted above her.

Insurgent made his way around the ringed corridor of the basement then turned right through the security doors to head under the plaza. He stopped next to Ira who was waiting for him at the lift.

"Aren't you taking anything with you?" said Insurgent.

Ira touched the locket around her neck that her mother had given her.

"Oh, I see, of course," said Insurgent.

Together they stepped into the lift. The aperture at the centre of the plaza opened up and the transparent lift rose up towards the underside of Matthanias.

"Once aboard, I will take command," said Insurgent.

"Yes, sir."

"There are no protocols for an event such as this, so we will pretty much be making it up as we go along. You happy with that?"

"Yes, sir."

CHAPTER 34

UK: London: Stratford: The United States Interrogation
Society: Day 5

The paper ticket in Pete's hand had the number six hundred and one printed on it in black ink. The electronic clocks on the screens bolted around the upper perimeter of the stadium read twenty-two.

"They ship you from Belgium?" asked a young man sitting next to Pete.

Pete ignored him.

"Listen, buddy, there's no need to be rude."

"What number ticket do you have?" said Pete.

"One hundred and one."

"Number twenty three to the counter please."

A woman about a hundred metres down the waiting area got to her feet and started making her way to the front.

"This waiting room is huge," said the man. "You could host an international athletics meeting in it."

"That's because they did," said Pete finally turning to the young man. "You're not from around here are you?"

"No, I'm from Texas," said the man.

"Is that so," said Pete.

"It's in the United States of America."

"I know where Texas is," said Pete. "You however have obviously never heard of the London Olympics."

"Eh? The what?"

"What happened to your hand?" said Pete looking at the bandaged stump where there should have been fingers, a thumb, a palm.

"Oh that, that's why I'm here. I stuck it in that orb thing as a dare to impress my girlfriend. I nearly bled to death. You should have seen it – my arteries were pumping out blood everywhere, it was like some kind of zombie film!"

"I hope she was worth it."

"Yeah, she's gorgeous. She left me though. Said she still liked me but didn't enjoy dates where her boyfriend splattered blood all over her – not on a first date anyway. I think it was her favourite dress. It had polka dots and a low neckline."

"She sounds lovely," said Pete.

"Heh, that's irony, isn't it?"

"Yes."

"So anyway," continued the man, "the government shipped me here for interrogation. Pulling a stunt like that put me on some kind of list."

"Number twenty four to the counter please."

It started to rain. Pete pulled the collar up on his shirt as water splashed down around them.

"Well," said Pete. "What would it take to get you to swap your ticket for mine?"

"What you got?"

"Six hundred and one."

"No way."

"How about an umbrella?" said Pete.

"You haven't got an umbrella."

Pete produced a retractable black umbrella from his coat pocket.

"Where did you get that?"

"I stole it from one of the guards on the way in. It reminds me of my girlfriend – she likes Mary Poppins. So do we have a deal?"

"Deal," said the man and passed his ticket over.

"Number twenty five to the counter please."

Hours later it had grown dark. Pete was completely drenched. Throughout the day Matthanias had touched down in the centre of the stadium, a group of prisoners would march in and then it would lift off again into the air. People were applauding each time for some strange reason. Pete's friend was no more – once the guards spotted him sheltering

114

under the umbrella they'd dragged him off screaming. That was four hours ago. Pete hadn't seen him since.

"Number one hundred and one to the counter please."

Pete got to his feet and nearly collapsed: he'd been waiting around for so many days that his legs had become weak. Grasping hold of a hand rail he steadied himself and made his way to the end of the row.

"Excuse me. Sorry. Excuse me. Excuse me. Excuse me."

At the steps he paused a moment. Before him the rain-soaked stadium had turned into a mud bath. Matthanias shimmered in the centre: the rain hatching down and disappearing into its liquid hull. Pete made it to the bottom and a steward wearing an orange jacket directed him towards the check-in desk flashing his number. As he drew near, the lady behind the counter smiled, "Hello, sir. Name?"

"Peter. Peter Furst."

"And if I can just see your ticket – arh, thank you, sir. Do you have any baggage today?"

"What?"

"Any baggage, sir?"

"I'm about to be taken two hundred miles above the earth to be tortured, I forgot to pack."

"Very good, sir. Would you like a window seat?"

"Yeah, and can I have a chilled bottle of Dom Pérignon?"

The woman paused and moved her glasses down her nose. She examined him over the tortoiseshell rims, then set them back into position.

"Smoking or non-smoking?"

A siren sounded through the loudspeakers in the stadium. Matthanias lifted off the ground, trailing water.

"What's that noise?"

"That's the five-o'clock siren," said the woman. "We have been chatting a while haven't we!"

A steel shutter slammed down between them.

"Will all prisoners please return to their seats immediately. We are entering Family Protection Time."

"Oh for the love of God," said Pete.

CHAPTER 35

USA: Texas: Hill Country State Natural Area: Hermit's
Trace: Day 6

Inside the chrysalis the imaginal cells came together and
started vibrating to match the frequency of the radiation
emanating from the advancing orb.

And instead of forming over the winter months in time for
spring, the transformation to a butterfly happened in minutes.
Somewhere within it was the memory of being the
caterpillar. But now it had become something altogether
new. It broke free from its chrysalis and emerged into the
cold Texan air. Around it the landscape was barren, rugged:
eroded limestone rising in steep slopes. Pumping fluid from
its body to inflate its wings, it hung upside down above the
creek waiting for the moment it would be ready for flight. It
came a moment before the edge of the orb reached it and as it
flew into the cold air it passed in a flutter of wings safely into
the dense woodland within.

CHAPTER 36

And so it was that on the seventh day he rested from all the work of creating.

The heroic last stand. A line of Alamo Ranger security guards stood in front of the limestone fortress. Here Davy Crockett fell in the Battle of the Alamo putting this piece of land onto the American history books. Above the battlement: the Star-Spangled Banner.

The whole of America watched live on television as the guards disappeared, saluting as they did so. The sound of a bugle playing retreat accompanied the lowering of the American flag. The Alamo became dense woodland as the orb erased the heart and soul of America: stamping over hallowed ground, removing heroes, rewriting history.

At the Tower of the Americas, soldiers looked out over the Alamo city, the decadence around them in the revolving restaurant abandoned in the flight to freedom. As the orb ballooned into the tower it activated the lift sensors, "Hello and welcome to the Tower of the Americas, the best view of the Alamo city."

The orb now soared nearly thirty miles into the sky reaching the white band of the stratosphere. It had already eaten into the ozone layer and now was pushing ever outward towards low earth orbit. Below the Earth's crust it began reforming the upper mantle.

As the Tower of the Americas began to disappear, a two hundred and thirty metre sheer drop to the wood below opened up before the soldiers. Above them a ring of helicopters sent missiles into the orb each warhead programmed to explode just before impact to put on a good show. The sky lit up like a fourth of July firework display. The restaurant revolved slowly, moving ranks of soldiers into contact with the sphere. Each met oblivion as they discharged their machine guns: high command unconcerned as long as it showed the American people they were at least trying.

To the east, those in the city who had refused to flee had placed a cross above their door to save them from the slaughter: a sign marking them out as a people of God.

"When he sees the cross, he will pass over you. No destruction will touch you when he strikes," the priest had said from a television studio in Nevada. Others had promised it would stop expanding on the seventh day and rest.

They were wrong.

Many died.

America mourned and withdrew and began making plans to flee their land: an exodus to the stars.

CHAPTER 37

ENGLAND: Isle of Wight Penal Colony

On the seventh day, after Gabriel had rested, the purge of human faeces began at The Great Stink. The Fletcher droids tunnelled through the solid shit like moles, eventually docking in the outer wall. Their red eyes flickered and went dark. Far off Gabriel could hear the rush of water coming from a great distance as if a dam had burst.

A jolt as everything shifted. Sensors along the wall flickered into life sending signals to the blades of the macerators placed every hundred metres throughout the cavity.

Gabriel pondered on his situation. It felt as if the penal colony was some automated mechanism to bring divine retribution – everybody within the cells would at some point end up here. They would be washed away, sliced and diced like rats dropped into a blender.

When the water hit Gabriel he tumbled backwards in the flow towards the steel blades of one of the macerators. He could hear it turning, spinning. As it reached its maximum speed the teeth became as one and the stove, plastic pigs, three dead rats, and Adriana Karembeu disappeared in an instant. Opening his eyes Gabriel saw the dead bodies of his two cell mates hit the whirl of metal. Their blood swirled towards him for a moment in the turbulence before being sucked back again through the rotating blades.

On the coastline the impellers pulled them towards the discharge pipe in the chalk cliff and spewed their diced remains into the choppy waters of the English Channel. Fish swam through the effluent, gorging.

Gabriel glanced around and then grabbed hold of a sluice gate wheel protruding from the ceiling. He held on as the water continued to thunder past. The noise was deafening. The force like being hit by the shockwave from a depth charge exploding. Gabriel struggled with his severed fingers. They had grown enough to allow him to grip, but not enough for this onslaught. One of his hands suddenly jerked away from the sluice wheel. His body arced backwards taking his feet dangerously close to the macerator. Straining he swung himself back and took hold again with both hands.

Through the noise, the stink and the pain Gabriel pondered over the fate of man before him. He had heard the cries as San Antonio was taken, its population of over a million cast from their homes.

Gabriel felt small bits of bone cut his side as the water continued in its relentless scouring of human shit. They had brought this on themselves, this false Eden. And yet it could act as a modern flood, purge the earth of evil so a new beginning could start. Only God had promised never again to flood the earth. And they were only indirectly responsible. At its heart lay a darkness.

Images of underground commuters packed together, their sweat flowing as one, filled Gabriel's mind. Above them a great flow of humanity swarmed past the ticket gates, down the escalators and onto the network of platforms. Those before them screamed and fell onto the track. When the train arrived from out of the tunnel it hit a solid wall of bodies and came crashing to a standstill. Most had already been crushed to death before the impact, the rest died instantly. Gabriel sighed, in time Avodah would corner mankind on the last piece of earth – then there would be nowhere to hide as the population converged. It would either be the best moment in man's history as they accepted defeat gracefully and without fear or they would tear themselves apart like animals. Gabriel feared it would be the latter.

Joshua Angerstein would face it with faith though. He would start there.

When the water subsided, Gabriel dropped to the floor and fell to his knees. He was physically exhausted, soaked and emotionally drained. Yet something had changed within him whilst he had been suspended in the worst of humanity's outpourings. Some of his strength from the old days, before he'd absorbed the blast of the premature death of the sun, had returned: rekindled by the faith of a small boy. He could sense the colour of belief seeping into him from the future as if it were a peach ripening in the summer sun.

Looking upwards he closed his eyes, "Lord, forgive me."

Maybe in Joshua there could be a point to it all after all.

As he prepared to walk back up the tunnel to find the exit, to slip unseen past the new intake of prisoners, the drying fans started up suddenly and with such force that Gabriel was caught off balance. He flew backwards into the rotating blades of the macerator. It took him and cut him into a million pieces.

Out to sea they lifted in the air like confetti over the chalk sea stacks. Seagulls gathered and began feasting in a squabble of feathers and beak. At the edge of the cliff a dandelion released a single seed to the air.

Later the light shafts of the Needle's red and white lighthouse illuminated the remaining ash as it hovered over the waters.

CHAPTER 38

Everybody is afraid of dying,
even Joshua Angerstein.
When you are young the fear,
is almost undetectable.
But it is still there waiting to grow,
to be fed.
An inconvenient truth,
a bloody nuisance.

CHAPTER 39

USA: Texas: Medina Valley: Utopia: Day 10

The sign on Recreational Road 1050 read:

> Welcome to Utopia: Population 373

Although today that is no longer true.

Instead if you were to follow the double yellow line in the centre of the road you'd turn right onto Houston Street and arrive at the edge of the orb.

If you tried to pass through to eat homemade pies at The Lost Maples cafe or to join the men in the backroom of Utopia's General Store to discuss the business of the day over coffee you would simply cease to exist. Within, the Blue Bell ice cream, homemade jerky and hand-trimmed steaks have become beetles, worms, mushrooms and moss.

For inside the orb is paradise. At its edge the cracked tarmac at your feet has changed into a carpet of bluebells winding into Mamre Wood like a river. You would stand breathless there at the world before you, listening to birdsong and the music of water on rock, your heart fluttering, your desire to be reborn.

And you'd see sunlight, glorious sunlight instead of the light from the moon. A fresh breeze would touch your cheeks as laughter and joy welled up within you. It would occur to you that the sphere was in fact a whole lot larger than the problems behind you and that your last ten years had deposited something bitter within your heart.

You'd think you would turn and run, your instinct for survival taking you back to the Sabinal River.

But no.

You are still there now.

You have been here for the last five minutes.

It starts to rain within Avodah.

You open your arms wide, close your eyes and hope that maybe, just maybe you will find a way in.

Welcome to Avodah: Population 1

CHAPTER 40

USA: Texas: Sabinal River

Joshua Angerstein loved The Lone Ranger. He'd seen all the old shows and liked to imagine that his dad was The Lone Ranger, that his dad could make everything okay in the world however dark or confusing things became.

The truth however was that a year ago he had received news that his dad had died in a skiing accident in Kitzbühel, Austria. It had shaken his world. He had once watched a film at school about American school children being told to hide under their desks in the event of an atomic strike. Duck and Cover they had called it, "Be sure and remember what Burt the Turtle just did friends. Duck and Cover."

He was still hiding under that desk.

Joshua walked for a while down the canyon topped with pecan trees and then, feeling the urgent need to pee, he ran scaring the cows and sending birds into the air from the treetops.

After making his contribution to the Sabinal River he zipped up his shorts and made his way over the rope bridge, the reflection of tree trunks below him. On the bank he took out the cheese and jam sandwich that he had made at the house after escaping the fellowship hall.

Kingfishers dived into the crystal waters flowing over the limestone. Joshua felt the smooth pebble in his pocket that his dad had skimmed clean across to where he now sat. Time, he felt, slowed down at this spot. A day here lasted forever. Each moment seemed to linger as if reluctant to move on.

He had first met God here, discovered a friendship that flourished in the quiet of the flow of water, a tranquillity where he could connect with all that was before and all that was to be.

His father had called this land, Paradise on Earth and Joshua knew his dad lived on in the soil under his feet and that his spirit lived in the trees. It was best when he was alone. He felt closer to him. He felt loved. His mum hardly noticed him, as if Joshua had become transparent after the skiing accident. She spent all her time campaigning about the dangers of keeping cows off the lower ski slopes. Little time then for a boy with all the world within. He wondered if she was still alive.

Joshua finished his sandwich, hid the crusts under a rock and walked along the riverbank to the giant cypress. He didn't have much time left now and looking up watched the dome eating into the landscape towards him like a cancer. Running, he reached the tree, grabbed the rope hanging from one of its great arms and prepared to launch himself back over the river. He had decided to defend his father. To do battle with the evil apparition before him. If God was truly with him then he could beat it, he just had to swing into the orb and believe.

Joshua first heard his mother talking about the orb with Old Man Johnson, who had got very excited and rounded up the inhabitants of Utopia and persuaded them all they should stay, that this was the rapture to the brave new world. He'd last seen them all in the fellowship hall in the Methodist Church on Cypress Street preparing to meet their God. Joshua's mum, when the others weren't looking, had slipped him out through the side door with instructions to get as far away as possible.

Now the running stopped. He would make his stand. He wasn't going to let it wipe away the landscape, it was a sacred part of him as it was to the Paleo-Indians before. And in his mind he was Tonto: the very best of Indians.

Joshua was distracted from his thoughts by his Uncle Wesson riding towards him waving wildly and shouting. A herd of cows blocked Wesson's way and his horse, Trojan, panicked and threw him as he pulled back hard on the reins.

Wesson fell backwards onto the dirt.

He lay still for a moment, the sound of rain drawing ever closer. Then wheezing he started to get up but found his legs broken. Joshua watched in horror. In his mind Joshua imagined his dad dying at the base of the ski slopes: the snap of his dad's neck as he crashed at high speed into the herd of cows.

"No!" he shouted as Avodah passed over his uncle.

Wesson struggled to move forward pulling himself by his hands. Gradually the orb removed his feet, legs, waist and body as if he were sinking into quicksand.

"No."

Gathering himself, Joshua waited until the edge of the orb was close enough. His eyes focussed and refocused on the motion of the river as the orb touched the bank. He blinked, subconscious minute movements within his eye kept him focused on the rain falling within the sphere. His body aligned itself in the direction of his gaze making small adjustments, preparing for the leap.

With a shout of, "Hi ho Silver, away!" Joshua launched out across the river.

The Pope's white stick flicked out before Joshua. Striking his chest, it held back the leap. Joshua fell back with a thump onto the ground.

The Pope extended his arm to help Joshua up.

Above them the liquid hull of Matthanias reflected the globe moving towards them.

"Come," said the Pope. "Today you do not die."

CHAPTER 41

Low Earth Orbit

The Cousteau Class Two spaceship circled the Earth, its parallax engines resisting the lure of the gravity well and propelling the craft through the Kessler Tube: a doughnut shaped highway giving clear passage through the space junk.

Constructed after Earth's low orbit became saturated with bits of old spacecraft, satellites, rocket stages, sofas, iron beds, condoms et cetera, the final push for the Kessler Tube came after the President of France was hit by a piece of toilet plumbing from the decaying International Space Station. His death had been broadcast live on air before millions of shocked Frenchmen watching the first presidential spacewalk.

The tube worked reasonably well as long as the spacecraft all went clockwise. Of course there was always an idiot who would decide to go anticlockwise and it was as Matthanias was doing an emergency manoeuvre to avoid an old Norwegian Viking Four that Insurgent slapped some photographs of Durram and Pete in various stages of passionate embrace before Pete.

"So," he said, "what do you – Oh shit."

Insurgent reached over to the photographs that had moved suddenly towards the ceiling during the evasive manoeuvre.

"That's rather destroyed the dramatic moment, don't you think?" he muttered and placed the photographs in front of Pete again. "Now, as I was saying, I must apologise that you were kept waiting before questioning for quite so long. Especially as you eventually ended back here again. Eh! Anyway, so what do you know about these?"

Pete blinked and picked up a photograph of what appeared to be him rolling naked in the grass with Durram, "They're faked. What the hell is this?"

"These photographs were taken at the centre of the orb that is currently heading for Houston and the Gulf of Mexico. An orb that if it carries on will eventually destroy the planet below us."

"That's not me," said Pete.

Insurgent placed Anthea Redfern and Bruce Forsyth on the table.

"Do you want these?"

"Where did you get them, they're mine," said Pete.

Roy Castle followed, then Jim Davidson, Graham Norton, Larry Grayson, Isla St Clair and Rosemarie Ford.

"These were stolen from Durram's flat a year ago."

"They're mine, give them to me."

"What do you know about the Convergence Project?" said Insurgent gathering them up.

"The what?"

"Did you kill the President?"

"What? Are you crazy?"

"Did you kill this woman?"

Insurgent produced a picture of Covenant looking exactly like Durram lying in a pool of blood at the Nautika restaurant in Dubrovnik.

"Listen, Pete," said Insurgent. He pocketed the trading cards and siphoned some water from the water cooler in the room. "Can I call you Pete? You have to understand that this looks very bad for you. The very existence of mankind is under threat and at the heart of it is someone who looks exactly like you and a woman whom you killed in cold blood over lunch. Do you see why we think that you might be the key?"

"It isn't me," said Pete.

Insurgent floated upwards and stuffed a cookie into his mouth, "Want one?"

"No. Give me my cards."

Pete looked at Durram in the photographs. It was her. He was sure of it. With him, or some doppelgänger of him. His heart thumped, he became confused and started to detach himself from the room.

"Well?" said Insurgent.

"I didn't kill her. I love her. The woman at the restaurant is an AI system called Covenant. I would never hurt Durram." Pete clenched his fists. "Never. Now can you please give me back my trading cards and make all this end, I can't take waiting around anymore."

"You're not going anywhere until you tell me more about this AI."

"She's a bitch, that's all there is to know."

"Listen, Peter," said Ira as she floated up through a circular aperture in the floor. "I'd cooperate with Insurgent if I were you. You see, here in the Kessler Tube, we are outside any laws that would bind us to the Geneva Convention."

"So finally we get to the torture bit," said Pete.

"Yes, that is why you are here and rest assured we will do whatever is necessary," said Insurgent. He produced the Anthea Redfern trading card. "This is ruined, it has a slight crease in the top right hand corner."

Insurgent slowly tore the card in half.

Ira raised an eyebrow, and then turned at a tapping noise on the one way window to the interrogation room.

"Hold on," said Ira.

She left the room.

Pete looked at Insurgent.

Insurgent smiled and offered Pete a cigarette.

"I'm going to kill you for doing that," said Pete looking at the two halves of Anthea Redfern floating before him.

"Suit yourself," said Insurgent lighting a cigarette. He breathed in. "This is the only place you can smoke now you know, legally anyway, the last bastion of the American smoker." Insurgent blew out a smoke ring. It floated across towards Pete and then, as Matthanias lurched sideways, shot towards the wall in a streak of smoke. "Those freakin' Vikings!" shouted Insurgent, getting up and pushing the intercom button. "Flight Deck, shoot the next one of those jackasses to kingdom come will you. Out."

Ira returned to the room and whispered in Insurgent's ear. He got to his feet, "Excuse me a moment, I won't be long."

"Where are you going?"

"Just wait here."

"No!" shouted Pete. "I can't take it, please don't make me wait anymore. Torture me, cut my hands off, whatever – just get on with it."

Insurgent ignored him and left, the door swishing closed behind him. Pete pushed himself up from his seat, retrieved the two halves of Anthea Redfern and put her in his pocket.

After ten minutes, Pete tucked his hands and feet into his body and assumed a foetal position. Floating up, he settled at the centre of the room and remained there, rotating slowly.

When the door eventually reopened, an hour later, Pete grabbed hold of the table leg and came to rest. The room appeared to carry on spinning and he watched the images of Insurgent, Ira and Steve McQueen blur across his retina.

"Peter Furst please," muttered Pete. "Peter Furst."

He threw up, sending globules of sick into the air.

A plastic sphere the size of a pea shot out from the sidewall. On reaching the cloud of vomit, it sucked it up inside of itself, expanding to the size of a golf ball.

The Pope struck it with his white stick as it passed him, "Fore!"

"Peter, meet the Pope," said Insurgent.

"You're fucking kidding me," said Pete wiping his mouth.

"Language please, Peter. You are in the presence of the most holy of men."

"Please," said the Pope. "Don't worry about it. I understand that you are a man of the cloth, Pete. You must come and visit the Vatican when this is all over, have a drink on the house."

The Pope placed Pete's trading card set on the table and pushed them over to him. "Yours I think."

Pete started arranging them in alphabetical order. "Why are you here?" he asked without looking up.

"One thing I've learnt over the years," said the Pope, "is that it's not the amount of running around you do that counts, it's being in the right place at the right time and knowing what to do. It stops you looking like an idiot and gives you time to enjoy life a little."

Pete took Jim Davidson and slipped him under Isla St Clair. The Pope looked out: his eyes unfocussed, seeing nothing, feeling everything.

"Don't you think we should enjoy our brief time in this life?" asked the Pope.

Pete took the two halves of Anthea Redfern from his pocket and placed them on the table.

"May I?" said the Pope and picked them up before Pete could respond. Holding them to his lips, he kissed the card and then returned it to Pete. The two halves had become one.

"You know what I'm talking about," said the Pope as Pete examined the card. "You learnt that in Dubrovnik. Why do you think you were sent there?"

"To kill myself for what I did. How did you just do that?"

The Pope leant forward and touched Pete on the shoulder, "A sleight of hand. Now forgive yourself, Pete. That was all in the past, you have to move on."

"And by move on you mean forget Durram?"

"No, Pete. You have been positioned at exactly the right place in the story, you have to act, seize the moment."

"What am I supposed to do?"

"Go to her, Pete. Go to her."

Silence.

"Dry roasted peanut?" said the Pope offering the bag to Pete.

"Thanks," said Pete finally looking up. "And thanks for my cards."

The Pope smiled and taking Ira aside asked her if she wouldn't mind showing a rather excited and confused young man by the name of Joshua Angerstein around the ship.

CHAPTER 42

The man and the woman sit under the Dandelion Tree, its shade protecting their naked skin from the sun's rays. Durram has become Rebekah. Pete is Isaac.

Rebekah looked at the bunch of bluebells that Isaac held out to her. They were glistening with dew.

"Should we be cutting them? Aren't bluebells a protected species?"

"It's fine," said Isaac. "The whole place is carpeted with them. And besides who's to know? There's just you and me now."

Raising her hand, Rebekah brushed a wisp of hair from her face and started to fiddle with her ear lobe. A butterfly landed on her shoulder, then rose again into the air.

"I love it here," she said.

"This is where I used to come as a small boy," said Isaac. "When I wanted to be alone."

"Isaac, when I dream I see the furnace of stars, the cold embrace of the moon, the cry of a child. And it always ends with humanity collapsing into a single point and becoming nothing, pointless, worthless."

"That's very deep, Rebekah. I dream only of you."

"Isaac," said Rebekah. "Why aren't we hungry?"

"There is no need for food here. All that we need can be found in each other."

"Pity," said Rebekah. "I rather like food."

Rebekah got to her feet and looked out across the wood at the beauty around her. "Isaac, I've been thinking."

"Hmm?"

"We keep having sex, right?"

"Yes, of course."

"Well," Rebekah sighed, glanced at her feet. "Don't get me wrong, Isaac, I love it, really I do, but don't you find that after a while it all becomes – well a bit boring really. Can't we do something else for a change?"

"Such as?"

"Go for a walk, talk more. Eat – why can't we eat? I would love a burger, chips and a Donald's Donut. And a Coke, ice cold from the fridge, in a bottle – it would have to be in a glass bottle – with a straw."

Isaac stood up and ran his fingers through her hair. She smiled. He kissed her, moved a hand down to one of her breasts and felt the firmness of their form. "We just need to be more adventurous – try different positions, explore each other in new ways."

"No," said Rebekah. "You aren't listening."

"Sorry," said Isaac withdrawing. "Sorry, yes of course let's make a list of things to do."

"You aren't taking me seriously, Isaac. And where are the children?"

Isaac hesitated before replying, "Jacob and Esau?"

"Yes, what other children have we got?"

"Rebekah," said Isaac. "You have lost yourself inside that pretty head of yours. We don't have children for another nine months."

"What? What are you talking about, of course we have children."

"No, darling. We don't. We just started out. The twins will be along at the right time."

"I'm pregnant with them now?"

"Hopefully."

"What do you mean hopefully?"

"We have had unprotected sex for the last few days."

Rebekah raised an eyebrow, "But I'm on the pill. I can't be?"

"Look around you, Rebekah. Where have you got contraception from?"

"Every time we have sex in the future I could become pregnant?"

"Yes of course," laughed Isaac. "God, which planet do you live on? I love and protect you, and you – well you have babies. It's been that way since the dawn of time."

"But I can't give birth here in a wood."

"Well where else are you going to pop them out, Rebekah?"

"Don't talk to me like that."

"I'll talk to you however I want."

Rebekah glared at Isaac, "It's like I suddenly don't even know you."

"You've always wanted a family, you never stop going on about it."

At his words the smell of rain,

a metallic hunger, fungal and musty.

The sound of a nursery rhyme,

sung in falsetto lulling her to sleep.

Durram wanted to cry in response. Nothing appeared in her tear ducts.

"Fuck it," she shouted at Isaac. "I can't even cry in this bloody wood."

She turned and ran.

Isaac watched her and then shaking his head, sat back down and picked up the bunch of bluebells. He remained there for some time before stuffing them into his mouth. He chewed, swallowed, got to his feet and then tipped his head back. A chilling laugh flowed out from him.

It covered the wood in darkness.

CHAPTER 43

Low Earth Orbit

"Now then, Mr Furst, I'm going to take you through the RUMI Test."

"The what?"

"You will be asked a series of questions. By analysing your embryonic subconscious decision process in coming to your answers we will make a composite map to reveal your brain's Fractal Pattern."

"Fractal Pattern?"

"Yes, Mr Furst, the brain is obsessed with patterns. Any set of choices will mirror your own personal fractal pattern, whether it be on a macro or micro level. It doesn't matter how small the decisions, we will still see the same pattern repeating. Think of it like a fingerprint."

"I have no idea what you're talking about, just get on with it."

"Good, good. Can you just reply with the first thoughts that come into your head, be as creative as you wish – amaze me."

"Okay."

"A man and a woman arguing."

Pete picked up a pencil and started scribbling an answer.

"It would be better if you just gave me your first thoughts rather than doing that."

"It's this way or nothing," said Pete.

"Very well, as you wish."

After a minute, Pete scrunched up the paper into a ball, threw it to the floor and started again on a fresh piece. Finally, six pieces of paper later, he answered. "A crack in a windscreen snaking out to find an edge. When it reaches it

the woman places her hand on the man and he loses control
and drives the car off the edge of the mountain."

"Sexual urgency."

As before, Pete spent ten minutes formulating his answer.

"Any time you like."

"I'm just proof reading it. Okay … Durram on top of me.
She has turned to granite. The weight is starting to crush me.
I need to free her before I implode."

"What a woman's laughter can do."

Five minutes of writing brought …

"Release a flock of birds into the sky. When they reach the
sun they cover it with their feathers to bring the night."

"The nature of true virility."

Two minutes …

"Teaching your heart how to fly by making it leap like a
baby bird from the safety of the nest within you."

"A thirsty fish."

One minute …

"A coin stuck in its throat. When it coughs it up, it buys
everyone a drink."

"In between stories."

Thirty seconds …

"A void – the vacuum of space. A netherworld where
mankind floats when his heart had grown cold."

"You're getting faster, very good. Next: An awkward
comparison."

Ten seconds …

"An author and his work."

"Birdsong from inside the egg."

Pete replied instantly without writing. "The Aztec god
Huitzilopochtli trapped in the form of a tiny humming bird
within the shell. He feeds off the yoke as if it were nectar.
When the shell opens he rises into the sky to bring the
morning."

"Thank you."

"Is that it?"

"Yes, thank you, Mr Furst. You have, if I may say, quite
an imagination. There is beauty and humour in your Fractal
Pattern that I haven't seen before. I see from your notes that
you used to be a writer before you became a helicopter pilot."

"Well that was a very long time ago."

"You should consider reawakening that gift. Now if you could just follow Ira she'll take you up to the restaurant at the end of Matthanias – you need to rest before your big day."

CHAPTER 44

Pete stood in the queue for a coffee on the rotating low gravity deck of Matthanias. Before him, tourists: many wearing white socks with sandals.

"So this Fractal Pattern thing," said Pete.

"What about it?" said Ira.

"Where does that leave the notion of free will?"

"Free will only really comes into play when you have two or more people – their choices no longer become the product of one person but mirror a coming together of their collective Fractal Patterns which can combine in an infinite number of ways. It's why it's never a good idea to have one person in charge. Our culture has naturally evolved to use the phenomenon long before we understood it – so we have marriage for example."

"I'm not sure I can believe that," said Pete.

"What's the matter, Pete? Are you afraid of some of the choices you might make left to your own devices? Have you heard of SANTA?"

"The game or the jolly old man in red?"

"The game."

"Yes, I played it once. I hated it."

"Well we made that, it was a by-product of our research into Fractal Patterns."

"Why are the military interested in that anyway?"

"It can predict the future, Pete. I know for example what you are about to order."

"No, shit – well that's hilarious, Ira, good one. By the way speaking of military – this is a military craft isn't it?"

"Yes," said Ira.

"And presumably we are in some sort of state of high alert?"

"Yes, of course."

"So?"

"So, what?"

"So," said Pete, "why do you have tourists on board?"

"You think we can afford to keep a craft as expensive as a Cousteau Class Two spaceship running without bringing in extra revenue sources?"

"I suppose you're going to tell me the ship has a gift shop next?"

"Of course."

"Only in America," said Pete.

"I'm sorry," said Ira. "But I find that highly offensive."

"Of course you do," said Pete. "On the plus side if you find any unexplored planets, you can give the paying customers complimentary red T-shirts and beam them down to the planet. Can you beam down zimmer frames?"

"Zimmer?"

"A walking frame."

"I'm sorry, but I find your humour a bit odd."

"And all this isn't?" said Pete pointing out of the window: an elderly man was jumping from the outer deck towards the Earth: a bungee rope unravelling behind him.

After that, Pete and Ira inched forward towards the till in silence.

When Pete was almost at the front the person before him took out a camera and pushed a few twinkly buttons.

"What would you like, sir?" said the woman behind the counter.

The tourist's telephoto lens telescoped out with little clicking sounds until it was inches from the woman's face.

"Sir?"

A white flash went off. The woman blinked and pushed the lens away from her face. "Sir?"

"Oh for God's sake," said Pete. He tapped the tourist on the shoulder.

"Excuse me."

The tourist turned to face Pete. Pete started to duck as the camera swung around towards his head.

Out of nowhere the Pope appeared and, flipping his white stick up, stopped the camera connecting with Pete's skull.

"Can I have a juice with a straw please?" said the Pope placing his order.

"Are you pushing in?" said Pete.

"I'm getting a drink for Joshua. Do you have an issue with that?" said the Pope.

"No, er – sorry go ahead. Here, I'll pay for a gingerbread man for him. My treat."

Pete took a gingerbread man from the counter display and placed it on the Pope's tray.

"He's not five-years-old, Pete," said Ira.

"Well," smiled the Pope. "That's fine. Thank you, Pete."

The Pope took a tray and, balancing the drink in the middle, made his way over the deck, one arm holding the tray the other tapping his stick on the brushed steel floor.

Pete watched, then turned to Ira, "If he needs that stick and it always makes that tap, tapping noise, then how did he suddenly just appear like that?"

"How would I know," said Ira. "But I do know that he owns the outfit running the coffee shop."

"The Vatican has a coffee house chain?"

"Oh yes. What? Oh I'll have a latte and a cookie, one of those ones you do with the little chocolate chips."

The woman passed over the order and smiled, "On the house."

"Thank you," said Ira. Nodding at Pete, she walked over to Insurgent who was sitting at a table in the corner examining immersion data predicting the orb's slow removal of the Earth.

Pete ordered whilst still watching Ira, "I'll have a cappuccino please."

Ira's leather trousers did seem a bit tight he thought. Blue lights shone up from the small holes peppering the floor under her feet. Ira passed a sign blu-tacked to the wall saying *Please do not use Blu-Tack on the wall.*

"Would you like chocolate on top?"

Pete looked at the woman, "No, thank you."

"It's horrible without chocolate."

"Excuse me? Do I know you? You look familiar?"

"I find a bit of chocolate hides the taste."

"Oh no – I've heard this before. Is this how they train you to talk to customers at the Vatican?"

"The Vatican, sir?"

"Yes you are employed by the Vatican."

"I'm sorry, sir, but this is Glitterbucks, we're not owned by the Vatican."

"Your attention please. Can all trained Q-One staff please report to the checkouts in the gift shop, thank you."

"Right, that's it," said Pete and forgetting his drink he stormed over to Insurgent's table and confronted Ira.

"You made me look like a complete idiot."

"Oh, really," said Ira. "Did I really? I'm most awfully sorry."

"Stop it you two," said Insurgent. "Pete, sit down – we need to go over this with you."

"Must we?"

"Pete," said Insurgent. "Sit down and shut up."

Pete pulled back a seat and sat down, as he did so he knocked Insurgent's Coke. It fell in a curve towards the floor in slow motion under the reduced gravity.

"Thanks," said Insurgent. "I hadn't wanted that, you go ahead and knock my drink off again and I'll have you ejected from the ship with the waste."

"Like a Coke do you?" said Pete.

A droid appeared with a mop and started cleaning up the mess.

"Now this," said Insurgent, "is the file we have on the Convergence Project."

Insurgent re-activated the immersion graphics, data streamed in front of them.

"I must explain before we start," said Insurgent, "that Ira is a Convergence Clone. Ira died two years ago when she was shot by a Family Protection Drone whilst on holiday in London."

"I'm very sorry to hear that," said Pete. "They can be a bit trigger-happy sometimes."

"I was accused of sleeping with a married man," said Ira. "For that they shot me in the heart."

Pete's eyes moved automatically to her chest. He could see the line of Ira's bra under the stretch of fabric. Her breasts looked a bit small. Pete imagined unscrewing her nipples as if they were wheel dust caps on a bicycle. He attached the pump head of a hose to her open valves and began pumping. "Well," said Pete finally. "We do take our family values very seriously. What do we have if we haven't a stable family unit?"

"Ira is my daughter," said Insurgent.

"Shit," said Pete. He put away his bike pump and dropped his gaze. "Look, sorry. Is this going to get awkward?"

"For the record," said Ira. "I never slept with anyone whilst I was in London."

Insurgent turned to Pete, "You can understand why I would rather have you tortured. The Pope, though, God bless him, has persuaded me that we need you. Now, Ira, maybe you can explain the Convergence Project to Pete."

"What do you fear most?" said Ira turning to Pete.

"I don't know," said Pete. "God? America?"

"You should fear yourself," said Ira. "You are capable of destroying yourself and all that you hold dear. It's a common weakness, the plague of mankind."

"Okay."

"What if when we die we fashion our own reality to retreat into? A world of our own making from our memories."

"What is this nonsense?" said Pete looking at Insurgent. Insurgent narrowed his eyes.

"Convergence," continued Ira. "Is a project that attempts to test that hypothesis. If it proves true then we are all destined to become Gods. I trust that even you can see that would be very bad. We believe these worlds are contained within Convergence points – infinitely small pockets of time all around us containing the afterlife."

"So," said Pete. "You have spent hundreds of thousands of dollars trying to find out if we walk around in an unseen soup of private hells?"

"Billions actually," said Insurgent. "Trillions if you count the research into testing the theory that they are connected with dark matter."

"Now," said Ira, leaning in closer to Pete. "What happens if one of those breaks into the real world?"

"You're clearly insane," said Pete. "I always suspected that you Americans had lost the plot years ago."

"Pete," said Insurgent. "Something went wrong with the project. The orb is just such a manifestation."

The earth appeared in the centre of the table, the orb growing out of it.

Insurgent pulled his hands apart and the Earth shrank and began moving in an elliptical orbit.

"We are no longer free," said Insurgent. "The Earth has changed course and appears to have entered into orbit around an unseen gravitational well. Calculations show the mass forming the well to be the same as our old sun. A sun that appears to be illuminating our little parasite here."

Insurgent reached forward and plucked the orb from it and held it in the palm of his hand.

"Welcome to the pleasure dome."

"What?" said Ira. "Is that what we are calling it now?"

"I'm fed up with saying *the orb*, *the sphere*," said Insurgent. "It contains constant scenes of a sexual nature. I think pleasure dome is a very apt way of describing it."

"Kubla Khan's sacred river to the sunless sea," said Ira. "Coleridge's poem – the fountain, wood, the caves."

"What?" said Insurgent. "No – I was thinking of Frankie Goes to Hollywood."

Insurgent placed his other hand over the top of the orb so it appeared to float between his palms. Then pulling them apart and twisting at the same time the orb expanded until the small figures of Durram and Pete could just be seen. Insurgent reached in and picking them up placed them on the table. He passed a Walther PPK handgun across to Pete.

"What's this?"

"When you get inside you need to kill this man, whoever he is."

"With that?"

"Yes, and then if that achieves nothing, kill her as well."

"No."

"Well you choose then, but I find killing normally sorts out most problems. It's them or most of mankind will die. Do it for the greater good."

Insurgent picked up the small figures of Pete and Durram and placed them back into the sphere and flicked it. It moved slowly back to the earth, then grew until it was all that was left.

Pete picked up the gun, "This is the best weapon is it then? You don't have a laser gun for me or something?"

"You're English aren't you?" said Insurgent.

"He certainly is," said Ira.

"Well then a Walther PPK it is," said Insurgent.

"I'm guessing you like films?" said Pete.

"Oh, yes. How do you know that?" said Insurgent.

"Just a hunch," said Pete and placed the gun in his pocket.

"Get a good night's sleep," said Insurgent. "We're sending you in tomorrow."

Ira's eyes flickered: her alert implant set to vibrate, "Excuse me."

"Of course," said Pete.

"She wasn't talking to you," said Insurgent.

Pete got to his feet. Insurgent reached out and grabbed his arm. "I saw you watching her back there. Leave Ira alone, if you mess with her I'll fucking kill you."

Pete tensed and felt a conflict of emotions within. Part of him was embarrassed and wanted to run, part of him wanted to strike Insurgent down for threatening him. After all this was the man who had found a weakness within him with his trading cards. The man who had torn Anthea Redfern in half. And how the hell had he known the significance of the cards? Just who was he?

Outside the orange hull of a Belgian spaceship passed slowly by. Dwarfing Matthanias it was the first wave of a fleet of ships taking eleven million Belgians to safety. Ever since their tourist trade had collapsed when Britain had decided to use their country as a propaganda tool to conjure up a bogeyman, they had diverted all their expertise and finance into leaving. That was decades ago, now they found themselves in the fortuitous position of being ready to leave just as things were looking somewhat dicey for planet Earth.

"Your attention please. Can all military personnel please report to their stations, thank you."

"Excuse me," said Insurgent looking at the Belgian ship. Getting up, he pushed past.

Pete stood there looking at Insurgent's back and imagined firing flaming arrows tipped in poison between his shoulder blades.

CHAPTER 45

When the Pope reached the table next to the window, he set the tray in front of Joshua Angerstein and sat himself down. Joshua took the gingerbread man and drink, smiled and started slurping through the straw.

They sat without speaking: Joshua quenching his thirst for fluid and sugar, the Pope listening to Noah and The Whale in his music implant.

Ten minutes later Joshua pushed the empty glass forward and smiled.

"You saved me."

"I did."

"I don't understand?"

"Well," said the Pope. "I think you of all people should be able to answer that."

"What do you mean?"

"You feel him in your heart don't you?"

"Yes."

"Well that's where God talks to me," said the Pope. "In my heart. That's how I knew I had to be there at that precise moment. You are a very important young man, do you know that?"

"So do you actually believe?" said Joshua. "Like for real?"

The Pope laughed, "I believe on a good day but there is always doubt. But that is good. It reminds me – sorry, Pete, won't you join us? It reminds me that I can't understand everything."

Pete sat down next to the Pope.

"Do you wish you could see again?" said Joshua.

"Every day."

"Doesn't that confuse you that God doesn't heal you?"

"Of course," said the Pope. "But blindness allows me to see in my imagination. That is far more powerful than any external stimulus. And besides, it keeps me focused or I'd be spending all my time looking at the pretty girl at the coffee shop as you are doing."

Joshua looked at his feet.

"Sorry, I have embarrassed you. That was not my intention."

"Look," said Pete. "What did you want?"

"I would like you to sit with us, Pete."

"Can you tell me one of your famous stories," said Joshua to the Pope. "I'd love to hear one, I've listened to all the podcasts."

"Of course," said the Pope. "It would be my pleasure. It's a story about a man and a woman."

"What happens?"

The Pope smiled. Settling back in his chair, he took a deep breath and folded his arms over his stomach. "A man finds a woman and in his heart he knows she is the one. He can see that she is strong and beautiful and full of grace. And when he loses her and all is lost he trusts not in what his head is telling him can't happen, no he believes instead in their story fluttering and pulsating under his skin.

"When days become weeks and weeks become years and he can no longer bear the pain he takes a knife and makes a small incision above his heart. A tiny bird emerges and hops onto his outstretched finger. The bird is weak but when it sings its song is so beautiful that whoever hears it is heartbroken and brought to tears.

"Each day the man places a fresh dressing over the incision to his skin that won't heal and each day he feeds the bird worms taken from the garden around the Lake of the Orchids. When the bird finally grows strong and can survive without him, he travels on foot to the top of Mount Penglai where the Eight Immortals dwell and the trees are laden with jewels. There he opens his hands and lets the story fly free." The Pope smiled, "Would you like to hear that story?"

Joshua's eyes widened, "Yes please."

Pete leant forward in his chair. Taking his Generation Game trading cards, he started laying them down on the table as he listened.

An hour later the Pope finished.

"Well," said Pete looking at Joshua. "You nearly had me in tears for this little kid and I don't even know him. Do you always weave your listeners into your stories?"

"Everyone is already in the story," said the Pope. "I just tell them the part they need to hear."

"And I'm the man at the start of the story?"

"Yes, of course."

"Can I have a look at your trading cards?" said Joshua.

"Yeah, sure," said Pete and passed them over. "Keep them if you like."

"Wow, thanks."

Pete got to his feet, "Thank you for the story."

"You're welcome," said the Pope.

Pete excused himself and as he left the restaurant he wondered how it was that he had just given a complete stranger his most treasured possessions. He entered the rotating toroidal lift running down the central axis of the ship. Shaped like a doughnut it was transparent, giving a view of the ship decks on one side and the empty core through the inner edge of the ring. Pete pressed the button for his quarters. The door swished closed. The Pope spoke from behind him as they descended.

"Don't hurt Ira, Pete."

Pete felt a jolt of shock: the Pope's sudden appearance like a grenade exploding. Air rushed into his lungs as he involuntarily opened his mouth and yelled. The metal rings set into the floor vibrated and rang out reproducing the scream at a higher pitch. His heart beating he gasped, "How did you get here so fast?"

"Never mind that, Pete. Listen you need to know about Ira's late husband."

"She was married?"

"Yes, a long time ago."

"She doesn't look very old."

"Pete, her husband was an Englishman. Try not to sleep with her, okay?"

CHAPTER 46

"So," said Ira, "I can either show you *the flight deck* – all very exciting … you can even talk to the pilots. Or, as you suggest, the gift shop – although I suspect a kid like you will want to go to *the flight deck*, yes?"

"I really would like to go to the gift shop, please," said Joshua Angerstein.

"What if the pilots let you take control of Matthanias for a moment? You could fly a spaceship!"

"Maybe later," said Joshua.

"Okay, okay," said Ira. "The gift shop."

"How much can I spend?"

"Let's just get there first," said Ira. "This way."

They stepped into the toroidal lift and descended.

Joshua watched as they passed the brightly illuminated engineering level, the Presidential suite and crew quarters. The next deck was dimly lit with flickering lights. Joshua could see shadows moving. Partitioning walls divided the deck into segments like an orange. The walls seemed to be moving.

"What deck was that?" said Joshua as it disappeared above them to be replaced by the holiday deck, the prisoner waiting rooms and then the press deck. "Is it where they torture the prisoners?"

"The dark one?" Ira laughed. "No, we call it the Gilliam deck, but officially it's the administration level."

"Gilliam?"

"Terry Gilliam," said Ira. "No? Means nothing? Remind me to show you Brazil when I'm off duty, I'll take you to the recreational deck and we can watch the movie."

"With popcorn?"

"Yes, the film won't work unless we eat popcorn. The energy of our hand movements from the bucket to our mouths is harvested to power the projector."

"Really?"

Ira smiled, "No, I'm just being silly."

"You're funny," said Joshua.

"Most people say I'm a bit odd. I like funny better, thank you."

"You look a little bit like my mum," said Joshua.

"I do?" said Ira.

"Yes, she was very pretty like you."

"Well, thank you, Joshua, I'm sure your mother was a wonderful person."

"Was?"

"Sorry, is."

"You think she's dead?" said Joshua.

"I don't know, Joshua," said Ira. "Let's hope not."

The lights counted down towards the lower deck.

"Why are there green containers stacked up on each level?" said Joshua.

"It's bin day," said Ira. "Those are wheelie bins."

Joshua pressed his face up against the plastic inner wall of the lift and stared into space. After a moment he turned back to Ira, "My Mum never took me to a gift shop."

"Really?"

"She said they were a rip off, that there was no way I was ever stepping foot in one – not whilst she was alive anyway."

Ira reached out and held his hand.

"So," said Joshua. "If we go to the gift shop then it will be a kind of closure for me – an acceptance that she died."

Ira looked at Joshua, behind him the lights from the lift bled into the darkness of space within the core.

"Sorry, how old are you, Joshua?"

"Eleven."

"You're very thoughtful for an eleven-year-old."

"God taught me. He said I was to trust him even when I couldn't understand what was going on."

"God eh?" said Ira. "Does he speak much to you then?"

"He used to, he's gone a bit quiet recently."

"I see."

TING.

"Do you think that's because you are a little older now, Joshua?"

The lift doors swished back.

Joshua looked at Ira, "No, why would you say that?"

"Sorry, look. We're here."

Before them, large spheres floated about the deck. Written on each were signs saying things like, *Space Junk*, *Kitchen*, *Toys*: each had three circular apertures.

"Off you go," said Ira.

Joshua hesitated, then floated out of the lift into the shop and entered the sphere labelled *Toys*. Inside he found himself within a small cavity with toys wrapped around the inner surface of the sphere. He reached out and took one, his mind filled with wonder.

An hour later Joshua made his way over to Ira. She was reading a coffee table book on the Chinese sect called *Five Septembers with Fallen Leaves*. In it was an account of how, in an attempt to prevent lustful thoughts in men, the women ate the Hoelen mushrooms from the base of Chinese red pine trees. A fungi that sought to destroy its wooden host, the women consumed it in vast quantities from the age of three and that combined with exercise and bamboo stiffened corsets reduced their breasts so they appeared flat chested. Ira made a mental note to check for Hoelen in her dietary pills.

Joshua tugged her hand and showed her his bag of gifts.

"That's a lot of stuff you have there, Joshua."

"Do you like it?" said Joshua. "I like this the best." He pulled out a metallic model of Matthanias.

"It's very nice," said Ira.

"I got you a Ripley Aliens sleep set," said Joshua fishing it out of the bag. "Aliens is cool."

Ira looked at the cropped white vest and knickers. It looked a little tight.

"Thank you, that's very sweet."

"And," said Joshua. "I've got a present for Pete. It's an apron with *Matthanias is Go!* on it."

"I'm sure he'll love it, let's get all this to the till shall we?"

"I don't have to put any of it back?"

"No, Joshua."

"Thanks, Ira, you're the best!"

Ira laughed, "Come on."

Twenty minutes later, they finally got to the front of the checkout queue. Ira started putting the gift items onto the magnetic conveyor belt.

"Would you like any help with your packing?" said the young man behind the till. He was wearing a T-shirt with the slogan *Air Force One : Do Not Be Alarmed.*

"No thanks," said Ira.

The man nodded, "Have it your way." He exploded into action: a whirl of limbs below a face full of acne. Within seconds all the items were scanned and stacked into the packing area.

"Would you like any help with your packing?" repeated the man, as Ira took the first item.

"Was it a race?" said Ira. "Should I have said yes? Did you go extra fast to show that I'm incapable of packing and you would do a far better job than I ever could?"

"Sorry, madam?"

"Don't worry," said Ira and stooping down to Joshua whispered, "Watch this, you'll find it funny."

"What?" said Joshua.

"I will now be asked questions as if I am a two-old child instead of second in command of the ship."

"If, madam, could just put her card into the little slot."

"What, this one?" said Ira. "I just push it in?"

"Yes, madam, thank you."

BEEP. BEEP. BEEP.

"If you could just type your number in please."

"What, into this keypad here?" said Ira.

"Yes please, madam."

Ira typed her number in and tapped her fingers on the counter as she waited.

"It takes a while," explained the young man. "It's hard to get a signal in orbit sometimes."

"Of course," said Ira.

BEEP. BEEP. BEEP.

"If you could just take your card."

"So I just remove it from the machine, like so?"

"Yes, madam. Thank you."

Ira remained floating in front of the till.

"Yes?" said the man eventually.

"Oh – I'm sorry," said Ira. "What do I do with the card now?"

"Put it back in your pocket, madam."

"Of course, how silly of me."

Joshua giggled, Ira glanced down at him and winked.

"Good job, you're here to help me," said Ira turning to the man. "Really I wonder how I manage to wipe my own arse sometimes."

Joshua burst into laughter, "You said arse!"

"Come on," said Ira and taking his hand again they left quickly.

"You're fun," said Joshua as they waited for the lift.

Under their feet a semi-circular glass window revealed powder-blue surgeonfish shoaling together to form complex shapes.

Joshua got down on his knees and watched them.

"What are they?" he asked.

"Beautiful aren't they?" said Ira. "They form part of the mainframe of the ship's organic computer. This window is just a glimpse into that world, the whole ship has a network of rivers within it like arteries all leading to the liquid outer hull."

"Wow."

Joshua pressed his hand against the glass. In the depths he could see a scuba diver swimming up through an aperture created by the surgeonfish. Light shone up below outlining the diver's yellow and pink wetsuit and illuminating her flowing hair.

"One of the IT techs," said Ira. "We've progressed quite a way from the geeky basement guys of old."

"She's beautiful," said Joshua.

"The world is full of surprises, eh, Joshua."

The lift arrived and they stepped in.

"Ira, can I ask you about the orb?"

"Of course," said Ira, reaching out to push the button for the recreational deck.

"How come it doesn't do daft things like making the Earth out of plasticine?"

Ira hesitated, "Sorry, what?"

"Or chocolate. If it was my imagination the sea would be made of jelly and I'd make the clouds out of marshmallows."

Ira stood there looking at Joshua, his words sinking into her mind like seeds thrust into wet soil.

"Are you okay, Ira?" said Joshua after a minute.

"Yes, sorry, I think we may have missed something important."

Chapter 47

Pete slept badly that night. At first anyway. In the early hours of the morning he dreamt he was sitting on a dune overlooking a desert. Cast-iron beds were arranged in rows in the sand stretching along the horizon. Tobosa grass waved in the breeze beside him. The sun bore down and brought warmth to his bones in the cold of the autumn air.

On each bed couples rose and fell in unison to instructions emanating from afar. Why was it always sex that drove the machine, mused Pete. And why was he here? He distinctly remembered making the decision not to leave Dubrovnik for Durram, to put her behind him. But he was here anyway preparing to throw himself at her in the morning. How had that happened? Was it fate or had he on some subconscious level made choices to bring himself to this point?

It started to snow, thin at first and then large fluffy flakes. It covered the desert, hiding it: rendering it invisible. Then from the west a great sea appeared. As it drew near, Pete rose into the air on a pillar of stone. Below him the sea crashed down and swept the beds off towards the eastern horizon.

In jolting movements the pillar shifted and started retracting back into the ground taking Pete towards the water. In its depths he could see two great monsters locked in mortal combat.

It occurred to Pete at this point, as he drew ever closer to the titanic battle, that he should wake up. But the sky became darker as his eyelids fluttered. Stepping stones appeared before him as the pillar drew level with the surface of the sea. He stepped out and hopped across towards a small rocky island with a shack at its centre.

Once at the island he broke into a run and reaching the shack in an instant he came to a stop. Taking a deep breath, he pushed open the wooden door. It made a creaking sound. The smell of burning stone curled about his shoulders. He could feel something behind him. Thunder. The crack of lightning. The chaos of movement from the two great monsters sent vibrations under his feet. Breathing hard he entered and slammed the door shut behind him.

Inside was a glass floor with a spiral stairway set in the middle. It was bathed in light and rose up through the thatched roof towards the stars. Pete put his foot on the bottom stair and started to climb.

Hanging in the air as he ascended were pictures containing memories of his time with Durram. Pete stopped at each and took in the scene recalling the smell, the noises, the sense of geometry and movement in each before moving on.

Three stuck in his mind and held him for what seemed hours.

The first was a picture of them throwing blue and orange Smarties across the room at each other which he remembered as being childish and intimate at the same time, as if they were sharing some forgotten childhood.

The second showed them decorating their flat together, he with his paintbrush poised ready to bring a Renaissance touch, her revealing her red knickers where her jeans had slipped. It brought a strong sense of sound, he could almost hear music and strangely, although his mind was full of images of them naked together, it was this memory that always seemed the most erotic to him.

In the third they were sitting together on the edge of the bed flicking through a cupcake book, their legs outstretched, their bodies close. It was the first time they had been on the same bed, albeit fully clothed and, instead of chocolate frostings, his mind had been full of the sense of excitement at their proximity.

Towards the top he finally realised what he was supposed to do. Turning he retraced his steps and descended.

When he opened the door to the shack a cold wind cut into his face. Before him the two monsters were still locked in battle. He spoke their names …

"Behemoth and Leviathan."

At the sound of his voice they stopped and approached him snarling, twisting, spitting. Pete threw open his arms and stretched out his fingers and thumbs. Blood emanated from each, forming ten rivers. Pete looked at the evil before him and then brought his hands together in a sudden movement, snapping the air between them.

A red shock wave of energy radiated out from him. Taking hold of Behemoth and Leviathan it pushed them back into the depths of the sea. The waters grew calm above them. It appeared as if a circle of glass were forming.

And then Durram rose up. She was spinning in the air, water falling from her toes, her hair twirling in golds and blues. Pete beckoned to her and she floated to him: her head tipped back, her arms open.

In the embrace he was awoken by the touch of cotton, the softness of breasts within.

He opened his eyes, half asleep, dreamy, thinking of Durram and looked into the face of Ira. She had slipped into his room and snuggled up within his arms. He could hear her breathing: she was asleep. She felt warm and inviting and full of promise.

Pete gently pulled his arm away and sat up. It was two in the morning. In the dim light she appeared to be in black and white. She stirred and rolled onto her back, her small pert breasts under her cropped white vest pointing towards the ceiling. Without the bed sheet holding her she floated up slightly.

Pete wasn't sure what to do.

Had she sleep-walked in? For fuck's sake he thought this wasn't fair. He lowered her gently back onto the bed and pulled the bed sheet back over her.

He lay there looking at her face and the rise and fall of her chest as she breathed. She was beautiful. He wanted her and despite the strength of his dreams recalling Durram, his mind become full of desire. The animal instinct to fuck such a creature, overpowering. It was what she wanted wasn't it, coming into his bed? He should wake her, take her and become one with her. And yet Pete couldn't shake the warning from the Pope and the feeling that she had arrived subliminally, drawn by some frustrated desire to be held again by her English husband. Surely within him was the goodness to lie still?

In the end he decided to take his chances, to gently wake her and satisfy the blood pulsating through his erection.

And then Durram rescued him, her memory calling him home from the darkness like a lighthouse in the mist. He could die tomorrow; this could be his last night.

He held his hand out before him and opened and closed his fingers, following the pulse under his skin. How, Durram asked him within his mind, or he thought he heard her ask him, how did he want to spend that last night? Pete brought his fingertips down into the flesh of his palm and formed a fist.

It was the first time he had ever sensed her voice within his mind. His subconscious was always so vague when presenting her to his conscious mind, like she was just an impression, roughly rendered.

Pete pulled the sheets fully over Ira, then kissing her softly on the cheek he got up and left his quarters. As the door closed behind him he looked back for a moment and then floating down the corridor he made his way to the observation deck.

There, as he watched the stars, a moment of clarity brought self-realisation. Left to his own selfish decisions puffed up by vanity he couldn't be trusted, he had been seconds away from waking Ira and making love to her. He needed something outside of himself to use as a moral compass – he needed the love of a woman. He needed Durram.

In the morning when he returned he found Ira gone, the smell of her still on the bed sheets. Slipped under the door was a folded piece of paper. Pete picked it up wondering if it was a message from Ira about the night before. Some kind of explanation. When he read the contents an aperture within his heart opened with a slicing action and blood flooded his world. He felt strung up, betrayed, rejected and alone.

The note was a copy of a letter from an abortion clinic in London, on it the name of Durram and her signature of consent at the bottom. Scribbled at the side a handwritten message signed by Insurgent.

Pete, In case you need any motive to kill your beloved Durram. For the record they were twins and you were the father.

At breakfast they served him poached eggs, cooked just right, the way he liked them.

A fitting last meal.

CHAPTER 48

Pete raised his arms to accept the spacesuit.

"Why do I need this?"

"We are going to winch you down through the top of the sphere," said Ira. "At its current height the sphere is skimming the top of the mesosphere so I think the suits a good idea, don't you?"

Pete looked into Ira's eyes searching for answers, some recognition of the night before.

Nothing.

"Why can't we just land and I'll walk in?" he said finally. "Why the drama?"

"Time is moving slower inside the sphere. Most of America would have been lost by the time you get to the centre to find them."

"Right."

"As soon as you're in, punch the keypad on your wrist and the suit will fly you down towards the epicentre."

The Pope stepped forward and helped Pete lock his helmet into place. Joshua Angerstein shook Pete's arm, "You're just like Buck Rogers."

"I am?" said Pete.

"Yes," said Joshua. "A hero."

"I don't think so."

"You better believe it, buster," said Insurgent. "America is depending on you."

Joshua Angerstein handed Pete his smooth pebble from the Sabinal River, "Can you place this inside the orb."

"Sure, kid," said Pete.

"And I got this for you," said Joshua handing Pete the apron with *Matthanias is Go!* on it.

Pete held it up and then folding it zipped it into the hip pocket of the suit. "Thank you, Joshua."

"Okay, Pete," said Insurgent. "Your Fractal Pattern results predict that you won't kill Durram. As you know I have taken steps to rectify that problem should the need arise."

Pete imagined the bullet in the Walther PPK piercing Insurgent's skull, entering his cerebral spinal fluid and punching a hole in his brain tissue.

Stepping forward he whispered in Insurgent's ear, "You bastard."

"Thanks," said Insurgent. He smiled at Pete and patted his back. "Off you go."

Pete stepped into Matthanias' airlock. He glanced back at Ira, "You don't remember anything?"

"Sorry?"

"Never mind."

The door behind him rolled across. He could see the Pope, Joshua Angerstein, Ira and Insurgent through the airlock's small circular window. Joshua Angerstein smiled, waved and mouthed, pebble, to him.

Insurgent spoke through the intercom inside Pete's helmet. "If the Pope is right then Durram may allow you through. If when we lower you, your feet disappear then give us the thumbs down and we will winch you back up to safety."

"Did you just say if my feet disappear?" said Pete, remembering his conversation with the Texan at The United States Interrogation Society:

"*I nearly bled to death. You should have seen it – my arteries were pumping out blood everywhere, it was like some kind of zombie film!*"

"Yes and Pete–"

"What?"

"Good luck, may God be with you."

The outside door to the airlock rotated back. Before him Pete could see the curvature of the orb. It was vast, bulging out of the earth. Around him buttons flashed, sensors checking everything was in order. Pete inched forward and swung his feet over the edge of the airlock.

"This isn't going to work," said Ira.

"Have faith," said the Pope.

Pete looked at the beauty of the earth: a cradle for life cushioned in blue and white. And he knew in that moment he had already forgiven her. She must have fallen pregnant just before they split up when they had disagreed over when to have children. Pete wondered if she had known she was pregnant when they had argued using the Larry Grayson issue as a screen to bring deeper issues to the surface. God, he thought, they must have kept the twins alive whilst she was in the coma. He thought back to his visit to her in hospital, she showed no signs of pregnancy but if she was …Pete did the maths … if she was five months pregnant then she may not have developed a bump yet. Why? That was the question that burned into his soul like a firebrand. She had wanted kids, she had wanted kids for as long as Pete had known her. Why did she abort them? At five months his children would have had eyebrows, eyelids, eyelashes, hair. Pete moved from the world of understanding to the world of imagination. There would be a story as to why, he bloody loved her and nothing was ever going to change that. God, poor Durram, he thought, what have you been through?

Pete rocked himself almost to the point of no return, "I want to see her again. I want her back."

"Pete, you need to stop that. Keep very still, we need to avoid any rolling during descent."

For a moment Pete saw Durram in his mind's eye and he tried to hold her image there. He'd always struggled to do that, she seemed elusive to him, her memory flickering and transient. But in that moment, suspended above the Earth on a foolhardy mission certain to fail, he saw her as the distance between them fell away. She smiled and called him as she had done in the hospital. Pete locked onto her and held her tight: held her at the centre of all that he was.

"I'm steady now."

"Good, the winch will take over as you step off and control your rate of descent."

"Okay."

"Try and keep as still as possible and keep your arms and legs into the side of your body. Now you see the row of red lights in front of you?"

"Yes."

"They will come on one by one and then once all five are on they will hold for a few seconds then all go out. Jump at that point."

Pete watched as the first light lit up.

"Oxygen levels: normal. Pulse rate one hundred and twenty beats per minute."

The second red light came on.

"Try and keep calm, Pete."

The third.

"Ventilation rate: twenty eight. Pupil dilation."

Fourth, fifth.

The lights went out.

Pete leapt out towards her.

Inside Matthanias a red warning light appeared on the outer wall of the airlock. Joshua Angerstein was the first to notice it.

"What's that mean?" he said pulling Ira's sleeve and pointing.

"Oh shit," she said looking at Insurgent, her eyes wide open. "He's forgotten to attach the tether."

"No," said Insurgent. "I released it just before he jumped."

"What?" shouted Ira. "Why?"

"This mission is all or nothing," said Insurgent. "He's not coming back."

Joshua Angerstein ran to the observation window and watched Pete free fall through space to the growing orb below.

CHAPTER 49

Avodah appeared to spin around before Pete as he tumbled towards its outer edge.

Green data overlain on his suit's helmet streamed in front of him ....

Suit able to take control. Accept?

"Yes."

Not recognised. Please select an option. You can choose audio, phone, climate control, take control or other.

"Take control."

Phone selected. Dial name please.

Pete held his arms out wide, his brain failing to come up with any viable means to control his fall. What had happened to the bloody tether?

"Oh Jesus."

Jesus accepted. Connecting now.

Pete closed his eyes. He was going to die.

"Hello, Peter."

"What? Who is this?" said Pete.

And that was the last thing Pete said before he touched the sphere.

THE WORLD OF IMAGINATION

CHAPTER 50

The armchair was covered in cigarette ash, coffee and semen stains. It appeared to be collapsing into the floor: its wooden frame under the leather snapped, twisted, splintering.

On it, flipping through the television channels with stubby fingers searching for porn, was Mr Stone.

The chair beside him was empty as it had been for the last year.

Mr Stone hadn't spoken since that fateful day. He felt as if he was waiting for the fire to melt his flesh and to bring relief as he floated closer to the heart of a lost sun.

Mr Stone found a programme about animal rescue showing a small kitten being removed from a collapsed building. A tear ran down his face when the kitten died in the arms of a seven-year-old child.

A knock at the door to the basement brought him to his feet. He walked across the floor and pulled the door back against the mound of rubbish, piling it up like snow before a snowplough.

A delivery man handed him a box, "Sign here, please."

Mr Stone marked a cross on the form and took the package. Shutting the door he made his way back to his armchair and rocked backwards and forwards with the parcel on his lap.

After an hour he stopped, got to his feet, urinated over the rubbish then sat again.

The news showed an image of the orb eating into the shores of the Gulf of Mexico. Mr Stone picked at a loose thread on the armrest, unravelling it until all that was left was white foam. When he was ready he undid the string around the parcel and pulled back the brown paper. Before him, wrapped around a wire frame with a plastic foam inner skin, was his rat.

He'd found it half eaten on the rooftop the day they'd released him from questioning. It was a simple matter even for Mr Stone to find a taxidermist in the small ads who had skinned the rat and used its skull and leg bones to form the basis for the wire reconstruction. It had been harder for Mr Stone to save up the money to pay for it. In fact he was forced in the end to concede defeat, having no real income, and had sold his porn collection to the local adult shop. It brought in enough to pay for the work to both of the pieces the taxidermist had collected.

Mr Stone took his pet and placed it on the mantelpiece. He ran his hand down its back, stroking the fur, then walked into the kitchen. He stood there looking at the picture of the kitten, stuck to the wall. Cockroaches ran over his feet and slipped in and out of open bin bags. A pile of pizza boxes stacked on the hob reached the bottom of the extractor fan. Mr Stone wondered if it would suck everything out of the basement if he turned it on, not that he knew how to turn it on. He closed his eyes and saw himself being sucked up past the charcoal filter, the ducting bulging as he passed through, as if it were a python moving him to its stomach to be digested.

Tamarisk had allowed Mr Stone to remain on compassionate grounds – for a year anyway. The lease was almost up, the time for Mr Stone to be introduced to his wife almost upon him. He had decided this was not going to happen. Another knock at the door. Mr Stone wondered if it was the second piece from the taxidermist.

It was. The delivery man helped Mr Stone move it across the floor and after unwrapping it, Mr Stone positioned it in the empty chair next to him.

"Looking Good, Mr Brittle," said Mr Stone.

Mr Brittle stared ahead with glass eyes.

Mr Stone waited for a moment, then mimicking Mr Brittle said, "Looking good, Mr Stone."

CHAPTER 51

Low Earth Orbit

The screen rotated before Insurgent on the command deck. It showed Pete spread-eagled on the edge of the orb, the outer curve of his helmet and the tips of his boots within Avodah, the rest of his body just above as if he were floating face down in water.

At the same time as pondering this, Insurgent was also overseeing a last ditch attempt to use lethal force to stop the orb.

"You don't expect him to make it do you?" said Ira stepping up beside him.

"The Pope seemed pretty certain," said Insurgent. "And so far he hasn't disappeared like everyone and everything else."

Insurgent reached into the screen and pulled out the circle of spatial distortion time mines intersecting the ground around the perimeter of the sphere.

"Pete is a wild card," continued Insurgent, "it was never official. I have to proceed in accordance with President Kennedy's instructions to use any force necessary to stop the Pleasure Dome."

"I do wish you'd stop calling it that," said Ira. She pulled Pete out before her. "So he just appears to be floating there stuck at the edge."

Cupping her hands around him she pulled outwards and expanded his image. Memories of watching Durram and Pete naked together in the wood pushed to the front of her mind. Except it wasn't really Pete of course. She would never admit it but she did find him attractive, although she suspected that he was unaware that he was good looking: he seemed unsure of himself and slightly awkward as if he was afraid of something. Joshua appeared to like him, in fact he couldn't stop talking about him ever since Pete had given him the trading cards.

"He is very slowly passing through it," said Insurgent. "Almost like he's falling into quicksand. I'm not quite sure what to make of it."

Ira closed her eyes. In her mind: images of herself flying over the ocean, her hair flowing behind her, her wings fluttering in time to her heartbeat.

"Ira?"

Ira swooped up above the Earth and across the sun, the light streaming from it reducing her features to an outline: a black silhouette against the yellow canvas. She flew back towards the land and hovered prostrate just above Pete, the beat of her wings sending a breeze across his body.

"Ira," repeated Insurgent. "What are you doing?"

Ira descended upon Pete, her eyes dreamlike, her skin tingling.

"Nothing," said Ira opening her eyes. "Just daydreaming."

"Really? Now? Just check the data will you."

Ira placed the image of Pete back and hesitated. Something stirred in her mind but when she turned her conscious mind to it, it fled, afraid at what it might become.

She shook her head and looked at the data stream showing the orb's status. "The rate of expansion has increased. And there are readings of radio waves and X-rays being generated from the sphere."

"That's bad," said Insurgent. "Are you sure? You seem distracted this morning."

"Insurgent," said a voice over the intercom. "Mines are armed and ready at your mark."

"I thought the containment net showed that there was no way of stopping this thing?" said Ira.

"Try telling that to John F. Kennedy," said Insurgent. He span the mines around so they appeared to orbit his hand then flicked them back into the screen.

On the ground, the mines exploded in unison as if signalling the end to a firework show. The spatial distortion technology took the edge of the sphere and extracted a fragment of space from the continuum and converted it into time. The edge of the sphere jumped backwards by thirty seconds.

Pete's eyes flickered for a moment as the sphere released him.

A cow that had just disappeared within the orb reappeared for a brief moment then disappeared again as the sphere carried on. Pete became engulfed once more and rose up with the sphere as if he were being carried by a great wave.

"I think we should leave it well alone," said Ira. "Everything we do is just speeding it up, look."

The data showed another increase in the rate of expansion. The predictive models shifted from complete convergence in six years to one. Insurgent pushed the intercom ...

"Get the President on the line, we need to get him to Air Force One."

"We are Air Force One."

"Don't get smart with me, just get him, now!"

CHAPTER 52

USA: New York: Central Park: Day 13

Bathsheba walked down the spiral staircase in her slippers, her dressing gown cord straining around her swollen stomach. Within the wall to her side a small bird fluttered inside the chimney flue.

Only four months now until little Reagan junior would enter the world. Bathsheba could feel the baby kicking within her womb. Outside, moonlight passed through the gaps in the kwanzan cherry trees. Filtering through the stained glass, it fell on her in colours of blue and gold.

On the wall a picture of her late husband Uriah, with his arms around her. She stopped a moment and, kissing her finger, placed it on his image. She had been a fool and now she had lost him. They had awarded him The Medal of Honor at the funeral. He was a hero.

It had been a bad time in her life, first Uriah and then Reagan was reported missing presumed dead – all the men in her life seemed to disappear in acts of violence.

She reached down to pick up the post from her New York Mets welcome mat. A puff of dust appeared at the open fireplace: its bricks cold from the night before. Bathsheba flipped through her mail. There was a bill, an invitation to an exhibition by the late Noel Fielding at the Yossi Milo Gallery and a postcard with a picture of one of the Texan State Starships. It had the message *Wish you Were Here* on it. Turning it over she read the message …

To Bathsheba,
My love I can't wait until you join me here. The view is amazing, the stars so bright. I know that you are finding things confusing at the moment but trust me

it's probably for the best. Looking forward to seeing
you again. I have a little something for the baby when
it arrives, I think you'll like it.
Stay strong.
Love
Dad XXX

So he was safe, somewhere deep in space, evacuated from
Texas by the might of the Americans. Thank God she
thought – thank God one man in my life is still alive.

Feeling better she poured herself a glass of orange juice
then climbed back up the maple wood to the bathroom.
There she disrobed, pinned back her hair with a clasp covered
in Japanese obi fabric and slipped into a hot bath full of
bubbles: her pregnant stomach pushing up out of the water.

The bird in the wall beat its wings against the red terracotta
tiles lining the flue. A cloud of soot and dust entered the
drawing room downstairs. It hovered like dry ice over the
Croatian limestone floor.

CHAPTER 53

ENGLAND: London: St Margaret's Street: Day 14

The Pope finished leading the gathering in prayer and got to his feet. Around him, sitting on the green benches of The House of Commons, were representatives from all the world's religions.

The scene had drama, thought the Pope. He couldn't see anything of course but he could feel it in the air. He always loved The Pope's Question Time: a tradition carried on from when parliament used to meet here before the government sold Westminster to the Vatican. The ministers had moved into the film set of the chambers built in Manchester; it saved the country millions and the lighting was better for television. The Vatican though had found themselves in legal possession of a building falling apart, with old boilers, plumbing leaks, asbestos and vibration damage from tube trains: all threatening to pull the palace to the ground.

The Archbishop of Canterbury chaired the assembly.

"Order, questions to the Pope. Mr Sam Turnpike."

The house jeered and shouted. Mr Sam Turnpike got to his feet.

"Thank you, my question to the Prime Minister is this. Why have you pushed through the so-called pavement tax? A tax that demands payment from every household to pay a levy every time they have to use the pavement to gain access to their property? Isn't this grossly unfair?"

Mr Sam Turnpike sat back down to the sound of laughter.

"I am very grateful," said the Pope. "To my honourable friend but, as always, I must remind him that parliament moved from these premises a number of years ago and, as I have said many times, you need to go up the M1 to Manchester and put your questions there."

The Pope sat down.

Laughter.

A lump of ceiling fell to the floor sending a puff of dust up into the air.

"The Chief Rabbi of the British Orthodox synagogues," said The Archbishop of Canterbury.

"Thank you. My question, Mr Pope, is this. In light of the recent developments do you think a couple can be happy when they know this comes at the price of great anguish?"

"Ask a proper question, you time-waster."

The Pope got back to his feet.

"You are referring to the couple the media are calling Adam and Eve in the centre of the orb?"

"Indeed."

"What about the dinosaurs?"

"Your question assumes they are aware of their situation which–"

"But if they are?"

A drop of water fell from the wooden rafters into a bucket situated between the two opposing rows of benches.

"If I could finish, Ben. Your question is the same dilemma we face when asked the question, can a man be happy in heaven knowing that many suffer in hell? And I can't answer that, Ben, as well you know."

"Can God make a rock so big he can't lift it?"

The Chief Rabbi took a step forward, his feet passing the red line in the carpet.

"Howzat! He's out," said The Secretary General of the World Muslim League. "Get back to the pavilion you stupid old fool."

"Can the Chief Rabbi please take a step back," said The Archbishop of Canterbury. "The Secretary General of the World Muslim League."

"Thank you. Does the Pope intend to stay with his people if the orb continues to expand out across the Earth? Or does he intend to flee with the Americans who even now are preparing their exodus?"

"Thank you, for your question, Ali. And I look forward to asking you questions when you take over the role of leading the Council next year."

The sound of applause mixed with booing floated up past tethered lights and buffeted against the lattice of light above.

"And the year after that," continued the Pope. "And every year after until I return to my maker. Does that answer your question?"

"It does, thank you."

Hot steam started filtering through a large crack in one of the walls.

"Could God bake a biscuit so large that it would crush the earth?"

"Might I just say," added the Pope. "That the Americans are not planning a mass exodus, such a thing is of course not possible."

"The Russians left en masse, why can't the Americans?" said The Secretary General of the World Muslim League.

The Archbishop of Canterbury started to protest, wanting to move on. The Pope held up his hand.

"It's okay. Let's continue with this, it's about time I put the record straight."

A hush fell over the chamber.

"Can we just clear the Public Gallery please. Thank you."

"Gentleman," said the Pope after waiting a moment. "The Russians are still with us. They got so fed up with the constant fighting rekindled by the resurgence of Reaganomics that they made a deal with the CIA. They secured their borders, ran some rigged-up footage of them leaving, which the CIA commissioned Hollywood to make, then withdrew to their motherland deciding to have nothing to do with the outside world again. Why do you think the Americans patrol Russian borders? Nobody has set foot on Russian soil apart from the Russians for ten years. The whole area is a no fly zone. It was all very hush-hush."

"That's absolutely ridiculous," said The Secretary General of the World Muslim League.

"And believing that the Russians shipped one hundred and fifty million people into space isn't?"

"Well–"

"Of course the CIA kept Reagan in the dark over it, he hated the Russians. Come on where were the stars in the footage of their spaceships passing the moon?"

"He has a point," said Mr Sam Turnpike.

"Shut up will you," said The Chief Rabbi of the British Orthodox synagogues. "You're not even supposed to be here."

"What about the Belgians?"

The electricity failed. The chamber became dark, then the clunking of the back-up generators began clanging under their feet. The lights flickered back on.

"Ladies and Gentleman, please," said the Pope. "The truth is the CIA and Russia cooked up the whole idea because they both had a common enemy. That common enemy was Reagan. But I'm getting side-tracked, the whole point is that only the very rich and powerful can escape this, most of America will fall. The whole thing is a propaganda game they are playing with their own people to avoid panic. Most ordinary Americans are bulk buying beans at their local superstores in the expectation that the government will provide instructions as to when to gather at the spaceports. They might as well sing *Yankee Doodle Dandy* and put all their trust in a second visit from E.T."

A sudden burst of laughter. It ebbed quickly away when the chamber realised that maybe it was inappropriate in the circumstances. Above, the drip became a steady flow of water through the roof. A small explosion under their feet caused the lights to dim.

"The President of the Methodist Church of Great Britain," said The Archbishop of Canterbury.

"Thank you. Do you know what the government here is planning to do if the orb reaches these shores?"

"Current predictions, if it gets this far, is that it will hit Cornwall during the summer recess of parliament. I'm sure you can all work out for yourselves where many people wish the government would take their holidays this year."

Laughter, shouting, jeering.

"Order please," said The Archbishop of Canterbury. "The Dalai Lama."

More drops started falling into the chamber. A number of black umbrellas opened up along the pews like ellipsis preparing the chamber for silence.

"Thank you. This orb is a projection of heaven as fashioned by the predominant beliefs and thoughts of the couple within – a plane of existence that is affecting the whole world. Do you agree therefore that it will be temporary and will pass away once they move on?"

"Nonsense, Lama, mumbo jumbo."

"I believe that there is–"

"If God dropped a piece of toast would it land butter side down?"

A fire broke out under the floorboards. Flames flickered up through the raindrops.

"I think there is an element of truth in that," said the Pope. "In that I believe we each fashion our own reality as we die drawing on our memories of our life experiences. If we choose to dwell there in an introspective world of our own making without God, then that would be hell indeed."

The fire alarm started. A crack appeared up the wall behind The Archbishop of Canterbury. The chamber started to empty as people pushed and shoved.

"Whatever happens though, even if I die," continued the Pope. "Even if we all die – I will still believe and hope in my Lord."

"Sir, you need to leave now. We are evacuating the building."

"Of course, thank you. Question time is over?"

"Indeed, sir. Now if you could just come with me, then I'll get you to safety."

CHAPTER 54

Under the Dandelion Tree the two lovers met,
wonders explained, their paths are set.

Pete opened his eyes.

Looking up he saw the sun.

He was in.

He was alive.

He was hurtling towards the ground faster than the speed of sound. Across his helmet the message …

Caller not recognised.

Finally remembering Insurgent's instructions, Pete pushed a button on the suit's keypad and activated the suit's guidance system and rockets.

Looking down he could see the curve of the land below, the wisps of clouds, colours breaking through as treetops speared the sky. He felt a lightness within as if everything before had just been a dream. A sense of déjà vu. The memory of flying from childhood dreams: a letting go.

He touched down at the centre of it all where the great tree stood. There was nobody to be seen. He spoke into his intercom …

"Matthanias, this is Pete, come in."

Static. The sound of white noise.

"Matthanias, this is Pete."

Pete tried his suit's on-board computer …

Please select an option. You can choose audio, phone, climate control, take control or other.

"Phone."

Phone selected. Dial name please.

"Durram."

No networks detected.

Pete placed his hand up against the Dandelion Tree. At his feet he could see mutilated bluebells. His eyes started to flicker: he imagined he could see a young man standing at the tree. Voices, echoes in time …

ISAAC: God. If you're really there. If you really love me. Then move the tree to show me.

Pete looked up as The Dandelion Tree withdrew down into the ground as if being pulled by some ancient might into the earth. The branches folded up, birds flew from its grasp. The sound of marching from far away as if armies just out of sight were moving: moving towards him.

Pete's suit streamed information across his gaze ...

Precipitation detected: Snow.

He held out his gloved hand and watched the first of the snowflakes settle.

The tip of the Dandelion Tree slipped under the ground. A wisp of yellow mist floated up from the cavity in the soil. The overlay on his visor changed to …

Do not be afraid.

A red glow deep below shone under Pete's feet as the ground became translucent. Flames flickered. The sound of horses snorting surrounded him. Pete could hear swords clashing, arrows taking to the air. Then at the point the tree had submerged a great wind blew up from the hole sending the snowflakes spiralling and spinning upwards towards the sun.

Do not be afraid.

Pete dropped to his knees, trembling: his pulse rate dangerously high, a strong urge to pray, to seek protection, safety, security.

Looking up he thought he saw helicopters circling, each threading their way through the white sky. There was a jolt as one of the helicopters set down beside him and he watched himself jump from it, running, following a path set down for him long ago.

The memory of Durram's voice sounded in his ears as his teeth clenched. He became detached and joined with the elements around him. Snow flickered over his memories like static.

Then silence.

The soft fall of snow.

A dandelion pushed up from where the tree had stood. It opened its florets: a small cluster of yellow in the white. Images of its petals curling up and inwards flowed over the curve of his visor.

The suit's computer sensing the mood displayed ...

Audio selected: song: Tchaikovsky's Romeo and Juliet.

The dandelion became dark as its inner ring of bracts pulled up, cocooning the flowers within. It turned slightly and bowed as if tipping its head towards God. Around it a crown of outer bracts waiting for ascension.

Pete felt a tear run down his cheek within his helmet.

The bracts to the dandelion pulled away to reveal the white seeds. A wind picked up from the north and took each one into the sky. Pete watched as they floated upwards.

The last one remained for a moment and then it too lifted into the air. It swirled around becoming lost in the snow until coming to rest in the open hand of Durram.

She stood before him, holding the seed carefully, protecting it in her palm.

"Durram," he said through dry lips.

They looked at each other in the snow. The shade of the tree gone, the sun streaming down around them highlighting the moment in a solar embrace.

The ring of daffodils turned their faces towards the sun. Within them: Durram naked, snow under her feet watching an astronaut clothed in white with the badge of America on his shoulder, his boots sinking into the snow.

CHAPTER 55

A burning desire,
the heat of the sun.

"Isaac?"

Pete unscrewed his helmet.

"Why are you wearing that?" said Durram. "Where did you get it?"

"I've come to rescue you, Durram."

"It's Rebekah, Isaac – who's this Durram?"

"No your name is Durram. You've been involved in an accident."

"What are you talking about, Isaac?"

"Isaac?" said Pete. "No, it's Pete. Durram, I thought you were dead. When I came to see you again in the hospital … you weren't there, I … Oh, God." Pete placed his head in his hands. "Durram, I did such terrible things to avenge you. I was mad with rage."

"I think," said Durram. "That you have become confused, Isaac. You are ranting like a madman. Listen, I've been thinking about what happened under the tree when we argued. Let's just forgive and move on. You're right, I do want children and I want you to be the father."

Pete felt aroused, even in his confusion he couldn't take his eyes off her. Snowdrops fell and melted onto her skin, goose bumps covered her body. She folded her hands under her breasts. He wanted her. It had been so long.

Durram stepped forward and started taking his spacesuit off, "Come on get out of that stupid thing, this isn't Star Wars you know – this, if we can work together, is our paradise."

"Aren't you cold?" said Pete.

"No, I don't feel hot or cold here."

"Then why do you have goose bumps? Your toes are blue."

"Hmm?" Durram looked down at her body. "I hadn't noticed that."

Pete let her undress him, unsure as to what to do. Isaac? Rebekah? What the hell was she going on about?

Durram laughed and wrapped her hand around his erection, "I thought we had had a little chat about that."

"What?"

"Oh never mind," said Durram and then paused. "What's that?"

She ran her finger along the scar where his liver had been harvested.

"Oh, that," said Pete. "That's from–"

He stopped as the wound disappeared under her fingertips.

"All better now," said Durram. Wrapping her arms around his neck she kissed him. Pete stumbled back and they fell to the floor. The emotional bolts rusted down from the years of sorrow came away. He started laughing uncontrollably. Tears filled his eyes making it difficult to focus. His body shook finding resonance with the laughter. They rolled together in the snow aware only of the moment and came to rest with Durram lying on top of Pete. She pushed herself up and smiled.

Pete felt as if he was going to explode. It was all too much. To be with her again. The smell of her, the touch of her skin, the rush of being entwined outside in the open.

"Okay," said Durram. "Let's take your advice and get creative."

She guided him in, then arching her back thrust her breasts up. Pete could feel her muscles in her vagina tensing. Holding her hands out to either side of her, she starting whooping.

"Try and throw me," she shouted. Pete felt her squeezing her thighs into his side as she attempted to tether herself to his crotch. "Ride Em' cowboy!"

Pete thrust his pelvis up and losing all control surged into her, pumping semen: urgent, warm, sticky.

"Sorry," he gasped. "Sorry, it's been so long."

"Yeah, like an hour ago," laughed Durram.

"What? No. Don't joke about it. It's been nearly ten years."

Durram rolled off him and lay in the snow, her breath misting in the air.

Pete got to his feet, took a leaf and wiped himself clean.

The noise of a twig snapping under foot.

Pete looked up.

The doppelgänger stood before him, arms folded, watching.

Durram got to her feet, her mouth open, her gaze flickering between them.

Time stopped and held the moment as if it were cold water crystallising around an impurity found within.

CHAPTER 56

ENGLAND: London: Vadim Tower: Day 16

"Come on now, Mr Stone. Don't be foolish. Will you just open the door."

"We won't will we, Mr Brittle?"

"We won't, Mr Stone."

"We have a court order to evict you, Mr Stone. If you don't open this door immediately we will break it down."

"I'd like to see them try, Mr Stone."

"See them try, Mr Brittle."

"Glass of milk, Mr Stone?"

"Thank you, Mr Brittle. Why does eating chocolate, that's made of milk, make you thirsty for a glass of milk?"

"Don't know, Mr Stone."

"Have you got somebody in there with you?"

Mr Stone smiled. The floor of the apartment was clean. All the rubbish was stacked up against the door to form a barricade reaching to the ceiling.

"Your wife is here, Mr Stone. She wants you to come home now, you know the law."

Mr Stone turned the volume of the television up. It was on a split screen – one channel showing Bewitched, the other a Playboy channel.

"Samantha ... I thought you'd just like to know..."

Mr Stone passed over a bowl of Sugar Puffs to the rigid Mr Brittle: the image of breasts reflecting in his glass eyes.

"We like this bit, Mr Brittle."

"Yes we do, Mr Stone."

Canned laughter from the television filtered through the rubbish and under the door closely followed by the xylophone signature of Samantha's nose-twitch.

"Mr Stone." The voice of his state-enforced wife now. "Mr Stone, have you got a woman in there?"

Mr Stone lay back into the leather chair and unzipped himself, "Don't look, Mr Brittle."

"Not looking, Mr Stone."

Mr Stone watched as the girl on the Playboy channel drizzled quartz and dustings of coral and seashell down her bikini. A gentle breeze played with her hair, she opened her mouth and looked straight at the camera. Opening her fingers she ran them up her upstretched neck then made small furrows in the sand. A CLICK sounded as Mr Stone turned off the Playboy channel and she receded into a white spot in the middle of the screen.

Getting up he reached into the screen and pulled out Samantha from Bewitched. Spreading his arms apart she expanded to become life size. Mr Stone touched her red lips then ran his fingers through her bouffant hair.

The noise of the door splintering entered the room. Mr Stone clapped his hands and Samantha disappeared.

Mr Stone zipped himself back up and turning the two armchairs to face the wall of rubbish, sat back down.

A few crisp packets fluttered to the ground at the movement behind the barricade. Mr Stone could hear a gun being discharged into the rubbish. It bowed out towards him then sucked back into shape with a snap.

"Get out here right now!" screamed his wife. "Right now. Do you hear?" She hammered her fists into the rubbish and put her shoulder against it to push through. It opened with a rustling to accommodate her and pulled her into its detritus embrace. A muffled gasp. The soft sound of a scream. The wall shuddered and went still.

The credits to Bewitched started rolling to the accompaniment of the orchestra.

... Bewitched had been brought to you by the growing family of products of the Quaker Oats family ...

Mr Stone smiled, dropped two shells into his double-barrelled shotgun, snapped the barrels back up and fired into the wall.

Blood seeped out and trickled along the floor.

"That's murder, Mr Stone. Don't think you can get away with this. We will be back."

"This is the end, Mr Brittle."

"The end, Mr Stone."

"We fall together, Mr Brittle."

"Go out blazing, Mr Stone."

CHAPTER 57

"I see the government are going to introduce a tax incentive to keep a cow in your back garden," said Cardinal Number One.

"Why don't they just go the whole hog?" said Cardinal Number Two. "Ban cars all together, then we won't need all that milk they claim is in such short supply. They can start a *ride your cow to work week* instead."

Cardinal Number One finished his ale. "Another I think." He beckoned to Alessa, who appeared within moments with two frothing pints and some cheese crackers.

"Thanks, and I fancy a Coke as well."

"No problem."

Cardinal Number One continued to turn the pages of his newspaper. He stopped at a full-page naked picture of Durram within the orb. Alessa placed a Coke with ice and lemon before him and returned to the bar.

"Typical," he said. "We are possibly experiencing the end of the world and all the tabloids are interested in is cow tax and tits."

"That must have been one heck of a telephoto lens," said Cardinal Number Two. "Have you finished with that yet? I want to do the crossword."

"Hang on," said Cardinal Number One. "Here's a bit of real news, buried in the weekend section. It says that the American government is showing false news footage on ABC of State Starships evacuating Texas."

"There's no such thing as State Starships."

"Yeah, I know. Listen, it sounds like most Americans are going to die sitting in front of their televisions." Cardinal Number One read the newsprint. *"Our undercover reporter revealed yesterday that the Americans are duping their own people by imposing state control over all networks and showing mocked-up films of spaceships blasting off to into space from Texas. Most Americans instead of fleeing are waiting under curfew conditions for the siren call to alert them that it is time to make their way to their own State Starship. The elaborate subterfuge even involves sending fake postcards to people from their dead friends and relatives pretending they have left the Earth."*

"That's interesting," said Cardinal Number Two. "Now can I please have the paper?"

"Sure, once I've checked my lottery numbers."

"Oh, for goodness sake," said Cardinal Number Two reaching across to make a grab for the paper. There was resistance in the fibres of the wood pulp for a moment, then a ripping sound as the newspaper suddenly divided in two. One half hit Cardinal Number Two in the face. He fell back off his chair. Alessa walked over and folded her arms, "Boys, will you stop fighting."

"He ripped my paper."

Alessa removed the newspaper from Cardinal Number Two's face. It had opened out over him at the naked picture of Durram.

"I see you're getting up to date with current affairs," said Alessa. "Now if you could just–"

The phone at the back of the Vatican started to ring. Alessa brushed her hands down her apron, "Excuse me."

She left the bar area, picked up the telephone and rested against the loam walls listening. Every now and then she frowned and played with the tips of her hair.

"So we have very little time," said the Pope, "the expansion rate has carried on increasing and the magnitude of the radio waves and X-rays it's blasting out has increased tenfold."

"How much time have we got?" asked Alessa.

"I'm not sure, but it's showing complete convergence in ten months. No, hang on wait, nine months now. That's the problem, it keeps slowing down almost to a stop and then speeding up, getting faster and faster – there's no reason to it."

"What do you want me to do?"

"I'm on my way to brief the Prime Minister, I need you to evacuate the Vatican. Get everybody out and back to Rome."

"Very good, Your Holiness. And–"

"We choose to go to the moon."

"Who was that?"

"Oh that?" said the Pope. "That's John F. Kennedy. Excuse me a moment. John, the moon is ablaze with light, we can't escape to the moon, remember?"

A pause. Alessa watched the village cat curl up on one of the steel kegs.

"Sorry, Alex. He's newly cloned and still a bit confused. So get everyone out, and don't forget old man Samuel in the old forge."

"Samuel, I thought he had died years ago?"

"No, he just got tired. We all get tired after a while, Alex. Even me."

"We choose to go to the moon," said Kennedy in the background. "Not because it is easy, but because it's hard."

"Shh," said the Pope. "I'm trying to have a telephone conversation. Insurgent, can't you put him back in his box or something? Alex, you still there?"

"Yes, Your Holiness."

"It's going to get nasty, Alex. Before long there's going to be a standoff in Russia. We'll have a ring of European and African refugees trying to push their way through the American border patrols to a country most people think is uninhabited. The Russians have been in talks with Vice President Bush. So far they have said they will use lethal force to protect their homeland."

"What can we do?"

"Try and help as many as you can, be the calm in the storm. There is still a chance Pete can stop this thing. In the meantime I will try and save as many as I can. Matthanias can take a crew of a thousand. There are five other Cousteau Class Two ships, we will concentrate on the sick and new-borns."

"You still have some sway then?" said Alessa.

"Yeah, something God spoke to me about years ago, I didn't understand it until now. One final thing–"

"Yes."

192

"Save that damn cat will you."

Alessa replaced the receiver, picked the village cat up in her arms and made her way back into the bar area. She paused for a moment and took in the fireplace, breathed in the smell of hops, watched one of the cardinals wipe some froth from his mouth. Then with a sigh she filled her lungs and shouted, "Final orders please."

CHAPTER 58

ENGLAND: London: Vadim Tower: Day 18

Mr Stone remained in his armchair pointing his shotgun at the pile of rubbish towering up before him.

They hadn't come back.

From time to time, Mr Stone urinated and defecated adding to the barricade. The baby wipes he used solidifying onto the outer wall of the barrier: making it hard like concrete.

The apartment stank. Flies buzzed around Mr Stone's head. Mostly he ate Sugar Puffs from the cupboard that he and Mr Brittle had hoarded there in case of a nuclear strike from the Belgians. When they ran out he considered eating Mr Brittle but couldn't bring himself to eat his best friend, even if he was dead.

After a while he named the barricade Wilson and started having three way conversations between it, himself and Mr Brittle.

He lost weight.

He lost what little mind he had.

CHAPTER 59

The reflection of the London Bus in the glass of Sigue Sigue Sputnik Tower encrypted the advert into a cipher as if penned by Leonardo in secret. Or it turned it into drivel according to your point of view.

On the bus it read:

> It's A Naked Woman. Get Over It.

The words followed the contours of a close up of a pair of naked breasts.

"Got him," said the Family Protection Agent. He was sitting in his car with his partner, the image of the pair of tits behind them. They both looked sun-tanned as if they'd just returned from a holiday in Ibiza. "Records show that he is over twenty-five. There is no way he should be picking up passengers at this hour."

The taxi started to pull away from the taxi rank. The flash of the agent's siren caused it to come to a juddering halt. On the back window of the cab was a sticker with, *I Hate Cows* on it. The agents got out and drew their sidearms, "Get out of the car."

The taxi driver wound down his window, "You have got to be fucking kidding me!"

"Get out of the car, now!"

The first agent shot the back tyre of the cab, the second put a bullet in the fuel tank. A squirt of hot milk shot up in an arc into the air.

"Okay, okay," said the taxi driver and stepped out into the night air.

"Put your hands on the roof and spread your legs."

The taxi driver grunted and placed the palm of his hand on the taxi's roof, his other arm only a phantom now, its bones frozen in ice in Chukotka.

"Officers, we are in the middle of a city wide evacuation," said the taxi driver. "Surely to God the Family Protection hours don't apply in a national emergency?"

"Shut your mouth," said the first agent.

"You're stinking scum," said the second. "First we're doing you for working after five-o'clock."

"Yeah," said the first agent.

"Then we're doing you for profiteering during a state of national panic."

"Yeah."

"Then we're going to shoot you, see?"

"You can't do that," said the taxi driver.

"We can, see, because as you said we're in the middle of a city wide evacuation and so martial law applies."

A woman ran past on the pavement screaming, "Save my baby. Please some-one save my little baby."

The taxi driver watched her, then turning his head said, "I could have saved her – you've lost me a paying fare."

The first agent slammed the driver's face into the 'taxi for hire' sign. The second pushed the back of his gun into his head.

"We're going to count to five, see."

"Give you a chance to escape."

"You're going to let me run?" said the taxi driver.

"No, we're going to keep you here, count to five then blow your brains out."

"Yeah."

"Listen," said the taxi driver. "Can I make a confession before you kill me? I need to get something off my chest if I'm about to meet my maker. It was me. I started all of this. It was me who blew up the dam. I caused the orb to appear. I haven't slept for months. Every night I watch the news wracked with guilt."

"What are you fucking talking about?"

"My doctor has me on medication. My wife has left me."

"Start counting."

"Yeah, good idea. One."

"I only did it because I hate cows. Do you understand? I didn't mean for all this to happen. Really I didn't."

"Two."

A crowd had appeared at the taxi rank. People were lining up with cases stacked high, sleeping children in their arms. There was a beeping of horns from the other taxis waiting in the rank.

"Get a move on will you," shouted one leaning his head out of his cab window and shaking his fist.

The second agent walked over to the row of black cabs and started putting parking tickets on their windscreens. "You shouldn't be parked here," he moved down the line. "And you shouldn't and you shouldn't."

"We're not parked, we're waiting for you to get out of the bloody way," shouted one of the taxi drivers.

The agent ignored him and continued issuing tickets, "And you shouldn't and you shouldn't."

"Get back here," shouted his partner, "I'm starving. Let's finish this jerk and get a beef burger."

"Yeah, sorry."

"Three."

"Stop," said the taxi driver. "I've got a woman in the boot."

"Four, five."

BLAM!

The taxi driver slipped to the floor, his blood streaking down his cab.

"Great job."

"Another success for the family unit."

"Yeah."

"Better check the boot."

The second agent opened the boot and poked around, "No just a load of Coke bottles in here."

The first agent opened the cab door and peered inside. He spotted a passenger cowering on the back.

"Lovely evening, sir. Can I see some identification?"

The passenger produced a card from inside his suit.

"Travelling alone are we, sir?"

The man nodded.

"Without your wife?"

The man grimaced.

"She went on ahead with the children. I'm to meet her at Calais."

"Oh, I don't think so, sir."

"Am I in trouble?"

"Oh yes, sir, you need to be with your wife and children at this hour of the night, not stuck in the back of an illegal cab."

"But I must get to them, please."

"Step out of the car, sir."

"No, please,"

"Out of the car."

"Here," said the second agent. "I thought we were getting a burger and a Coke?"

"Hmm. Oh yeah, sorry, Look let's just count to three with this one and then we can do that, yes?"

"I ain't waiting any longer," said the second agent and leaning in he shot the passenger in the forehead.

"Right," he said scratching his arm. "Food."

"Yeah," said the first agent. "Wait, hang on."

"Not again, that's the third time."

"Yeah, sorry, I can't–"

The agent bent over double. Vomit replaced the mixture of vowels and consonants that had been spewing from his mouth.

CHAPTER 60

Eve lay on the large H of Tamarisk's landing pad waiting for the sound of blades to synchronise with her heartbeat. She was tired and numb: her emotions bleached out of her by a world hungry for gratification.

The shadow grew and the sky shrank until all she could see was the undercarriage of the helicopter. Dust flew up in the air. She rolled away and sat with her hands over her knees. Her hair twirled around her in the downdraft. She felt sick. She had been vomiting for five days now.

The helicopter skids set down and Servitude stepped out. Keeping his head low under the blades, he shouted, "Come on, Eve, it's time."

Servitude offered his hand. Eve looked at his arm. It was red like her own. Flakes of skin were peeling away. She grasped it and let him take her.

"Where are we going?"

"Russia, Eve. I arranged it with Insurgent after using Pete and Durram as bargaining chips."

"What? I can't hear you, sir."

Eve felt her heart thump as the noise from the blades increased. She got into her seat. Servitude reached over and passed her a fur coat.

"Put this on, it's going to be cold." He nodded to the pilot and they lifted into the air. "The Russians have a ship, Eve. It's all arranged."

"The Russians?"

"It's a long story."

Below them Angerstein appeared. He was holding his T-shirt in the air and waving frantically.

"Can't he come?" said Eve.

199

"Who?" said Servitude.

"Him," said Eve pointing. "He's my friend."

"Sorry, Eve," said Servitude, "The deal was only for two passes."

"But–"

"You didn't sleep with him did you?"

Eve sighed, sat back and watched London flow under her as they followed the line of the Thames.

"Are we going to be okay?" said Eve. "We are going to survive this aren't we?"

Servitude placed his hand on her knee, "What are you scared of?"

"Well dying basically," said Eve.

The helicopter turned at the mouth of the Thames and followed the coastline. Eve looked at Servitude, a strip of sand and open sea forming a backdrop behind him. The moonlight illuminated the breaking waves. Eve could smell the sea breeze through the open door.

Servitude turned his face to look straight at her. She saw glimpses of her past in the depth of his eyes.

CHAPTER 61

Bathsheba turned the fake postcard from her dad over in her hand. A lone figure at the base of the Statue of Liberty, she had taken an abandoned boat out here instead of joining the gridlock of cars trying to leave. Fires flickered on the Manhattan skyline behind her from the chaos and anarchy that had taken hold.

Everything had become so confusing. The power had been cut, the taps to her bath had run dry: nothing worked anymore. According to rumours on her wind up radio there was hardly anything of America left. The spaceships had been a lie; in fact everything in her life had only ever been a damn lie.

Bathsheba placed her hand over her bump. Her unborn baby within her womb had stopped kicking three days ago. She reached up and felt the scar on her cheek from the attack when they had broken into her house and desecrated everything within.

Taking the postcard, she placed it at the base of the Roman goddess of freedom.

As the sphere approached her, the Hudson River started draining into it, pulling the boats past her. The Armenian copper face of the Statue looked out without expression: the symbol of freedom blind to the changing world around it. The greens of the wood within the orb altered the familiar backdrop of a thousand million photographs. The sound of birdsong filled the air.

The smell of rain flowed around Bathsheba. She took a small pistol wrapped in the flag she'd kept from her husband's funeral. Three shell cases fell to the floor and rolled to her feet.

A moment's silence.

Her dad was dead, she knew that now.

They were all dead.

Shaking, she placed the gun in her mouth and pulled the trigger.

CHAPTER 62

ENGLAND: Isle of Wight Penal Colony: Day 40

The one thing that wasn't fully automated at The Great Stink was the great wash once a week. It depended on the one free inhabitant of the Isle of Wight: a man named Stan who had lived there for fifty years after being exiled for marrying a Belgian.

Two years ago Stan's wife had gone missing. It was just after the anti-aircraft dome in London had been destroyed and paranoia that Belgian bombers would blitz London had made life dangerous for any resident Belgians. They found her body the year later in the trawler net of a Cornish fishing boat just off Fowey harbour.

Stan wasn't entirely on his own: his sheepdog helped clear the cows from the old rusted hydrant wheel that rose out of the middle of the field above the prison. The cows there had become wild and savage and were responsible for the loss of his right hand which made operating the hydrant problematic.

However both Stan and his dog had fled just over three weeks ago in a little fishing boat to France. That meant the corridor had been unwashed and was rammed to bursting point. Many of the inmates had already died where effluent had oozed into their cells through cracks forming under the pressure.

Those still alive were among the few people still inhabiting the United Kingdom. The country had emptied as the orb had approached. Many had fled to Norway, none had dared enter Belgium even though it was rumoured the Belgians had already left Earth. The rest had invaded France.

That had been a particular problem for Stan who had left before this great exodus. When he landed at Omaha beach in Normandy, expecting to enjoy a lingering lunch of Caneton

Rouennaise and a bottle of Château Méaume, he was rather taken aback to be shot in the head by the French resistance. In fact the whole Anglo-French war broke out shortly afterwards – some said as a direct result of Stan's landing – stating that if the fleeing English had been channelled through to the French supermarkets as originally planned before the Omaha incident – that everything would have been fine. Instead the cross-channel ferries were met by the French army. This was rather inconvenient for the English who instead of passing through France in their attempt to escape the orb were bogged down in hand to hand combat around the Somme River.

The Pope, unlike Stan, did have two hands and a white stick to beat back the cows. And so after Matthanias set him down he made his way to the hydrant and emptied the great corridor circling the prison.

"Corridor, clear," said the Pope, the macerators vibrating the ground under his feet.

He pushed a button Ira had rigged up for him allowing him to control the Fletcher droids and walked down towards the opening in the ground near Carisbrooke Castle.

There he waited for the prisoners to follow the route King Charles the first had taken from his Isle of Wight cell to his execution. Today though they would, unlike Charles, be rescued by Americans in a spaceship.

If the Pope had known that the British Government would deploy them against the French two days later into the trenches on the front lines of the allied invasion, he might have thought twice. But although he was the Pope he couldn't be expected to know everything. And if you'd asked him he probably would have replied that acting in faith was the important thing, not the results.

CHAPTER 63

They'd turned off the electricity to the underground tunnels after everybody had been evacuated – although Adam Stevens couldn't work out why saving energy was important during the end of the world. Maybe it was just so ingrained in people that they retreated into the habit to stop themselves going mad.

Anyway it had bloody annoyed Adam – no one had actually checked the platforms were empty and that meant he and about a dozen or so other tramps were left behind in the dark. They'd shouted and shaken the iron grilles but their cries had gone unheard or just as likely, thought Adam, they'd been heard, but no one had given a shit.

It had been a long drop down the career ladder for Adam – once the president of Tamarisk – now, after the Trent incident, a tramp trying to keep one step ahead of the Family Protection Agents.

He warmed his hands on the fire. Its flickering light played over a poster showing a half-naked leather clad couple with the words, *Relax And Do It When Your Work is Done*. He thought of Eve and the sex. He hadn't had sex for over a year now. With Eve it had been like water flowing from a tap; now that life had run dry.

Women and children had sheltered from the Blitz in here and Adam was determined he would survive whatever Armageddon was playing out above ground. He achieved this by following a routine. The routine was everything and if another tramp, or rat, mouse or the occasional wild dog interrupted him he went mad and would tear his clothes, froth at the mouth and shout into the tunnels. He was, if pushed, a dangerous, crazy, fool of a man.

Today he had, like every other day, foraged early in the morning for fuel for his fire, checked his traps for food and collected water from the dripping pipes inside the tunnel at Waterloo. He'd also made up his mind he would eat Salient today. Sure he felt sorry for him, after all Salient had fallen from grace as he had, but he'd been dead for a week now and – well Adam was bloody hungry.

He would have to get dressed for dinner though – he wasn't a savage. He pulled Salient onto the fire, took off his own rags and carefully put on the guards uniform that was his formal dinner attire. After fiddling with the gold buttons on his jacket he donned his cap and straightened his name badge. It read … *Hello my name is Fred.*

When he realised he had forgotten to put on his black tie he became angry. The routine had been broken. Spitting and cursing he removed his jacket, kicked the half-charred body of Salient, grabbed a burning piece of wood from the fire and jumped over the *Mind the Gap* notice down onto the track.

He shouted into the tunnel to his right.

He shouted into the tunnel to his left.

Then he ripped sections from the *Relax* poster with his fingernails before torching it with the firebrand.

After that things got worse.

He ran screaming along the track setting fire to every poster until the wall was alight with flames.

Behind him the orb entered the station turning the tunnel to blue clay with crystals of selenite.

And so it was with a backdrop of blazing adverts, a madness in his eyes and obscenities on his lips that Adam Stevens died.

CHAPTER 64

ENGLAND: London: Vadim Tower

Mr Stone moved a forefinger up an inch from the armrest, then let it fall again. A puff of dust covering his finger rose up into the air. He was seated in a pool of his own urine, faeces and sick.

Why hadn't they come back? He wanted to fight them. He'd have them, he would. Have them.

Surrounding him were sewer rats. Hundreds of them. They'd eaten Mr Brittle and were waiting for Mr Stone to finally stop moving. They'd gnaw his face off first, then burrow in through his chest.

Wilson had stopped talking.

The wire framework of Mr Brittle provided an exoskeleton for the cockroaches which swarmed around within him.

The room was silent. The air heavy over him like a shroud.

When the orb passed through Wilson, Mr Stone gasped, a dry husky sound that echoed inside his head. Avodah was moving at speed, getting faster with every moment.

There was no time for last moment heroics.

No time to discharge his shotgun into it.

And so in an instant he was taken, erased and forgotten as if he had never truly existed.

Outside in the darkness of a deserted London, the glow of the dream detectors along the Thames blinked out one by one as the orb took them. The imported Eiffel Tower disappeared, the barking of dogs fighting over bones in the empty streets faded away.

On the open lawn in the garden of 10, Downing Street, the toys left scattered with only the echoes of children vanished.

The House of Commons, its inner chambers open to the heavens after the fire, became no more. The Parliamentary archives holding the bills for The Family Act and the Coming of Age Act disappeared. Big Ben became silent as it stopped half-way through signalling the dead of night.

It was part of the end.

The end of all things.

CHAPTER 65

The chalk and flint cliff towered up over the waters of the English Channel. Made from the skeletal remains of sea creatures that lived millions of years ago, it was now technically French soil: the English having sold it to help pay off their national debts to the French government. The Pope thought differently. This was and always would be part of England. He looked over the waters to the coastline of France, then upwards into the air where the memory of Spitfires bore down on German fighters.

Today the cliffs would provide no defence to England as there was nothing of England left. The Pope however stood his ground, the salt air around him and the sea breeze lifting his spirits. He skewered the last of his fish and chips with a wooden chip fork and washed it down with his favourite real ale from the Vatican. Dabbing ketchup from his mouth with a paper napkin, he walked over to the plastic bin on the cliff edge. It had the words *Keep Britain Tidy : Working together for cleaner, greener places* on it in green letters. The Pope scrunched up the newspaper and deposited it in the bin.

Brushing fish batter crumbs from his Steve McQueen T-shirt he lowered the French flag and hosted the Union Jack. It flapped and tugged at the flagpole. Saluting he turned and faced the orb as it approached over the chequered fields of green.

Above him Matthanias appeared. The Pope could hear the voice of Ira, "Won't you please change your mind?"

The Pope smiled and shook his head. "No," he shouted up into the wind where nobody could hear him. "I will go down with this ship."

"Please, for the sake of the kid."

The Pope stepped back towards the edge as the orb bore down on him. He indicated his response with a flick of his wrist. Matthanias withdrew.

He stood there for a moment, the cliff looking like a white ribbon of hope threading its way between the sea and sky. Before him the orb appeared as a sheer wall without end. Below ground unseen, it had eaten away and replaced the core, untroubled by the temperatures there as hot as the surface of the sun. Now at over twice the size of the moon, it was considerably larger than the Pope.

The Pope opened his eyes. Light poured in and for the first time in his life signals pulsed down his optic nerves. Blinking he could see a great forest as trees reclaimed industrial Britain.

"Is it so bad," thought the Pope. "Isn't this now a green and pleasant land again?"

Turning his back to approaching death, the Pope looked up at the heavens before him, "I don't understand any of this – how hundreds of millions are dead. Please look after Joshua for me, please don't let him die. I am and always will be your humble servant."

It started to snow, light at first, then great thick balls drifting down as if in slow motion. The Pope laughed, "Yes of course, how apt, snow in July. You always did have a sense of humour."

He closed his eyes again, threw his white stick into the waters below, opened his arms wide and accepted his fate – a lone figure full of faith and wonder on the coastline.

CHAPTER 66

LATVIA: Russian Border: Day 52

Snow span in vortexes at the tips of the helicopter blades: the chopping of air muffled in the white landscape. Eve and Servitude pulled up their hoods. Servitude started the ignition to the Ducati snowmobile and with Eve's arms around him they headed towards the border.

Before them the trees disappeared into the landscape as winter airbrushed all reference points causing Eve to feel light-headed. She imagined the world folding in on itself like an envelope to reveal hidden secrets written in the stone beneath.

The motion made her feel sick. Again. Servitude had given her some tablets to keep it under control, but she could feel herself deteriorating. Apparently it was the X-rays radiating out from the orb: burning her skin, churning her stomach.

When they finally came to a stop, the engine beneath her, she forgot for a moment who she was and what she was doing here in this foreign land.

Servitude produced their false identification papers provided by Insurgent and passed them to the border guards.

Eve looked at their white camouflage suits and the small red stars embossed with a hammer and sickle on their winter caps. Behind them she could see smoke spiralling up into the sky. The smell of burnt flesh filled her nostrils.

When the border guard produced a Makarov pistol and shot Servitude in the forehead, she disarmed the guard, kicked him in the leg and, taking control of the snowmobile, sped away.

One of the Russians placed a hand on the guard who had killed Servitude, then brought his fist to his chest, "Ya amirikanets!"

They laughed and took chase on snowmobiles past the burning remains of the American border guards.

Eve glanced behind her at the sound of their engines and throttled up to maximum speed. The snowmobile bounced over the topography outlining it in motion. Eve's heart rate increased. Her mind circled through her options as if trying to burrow through steel. They were getting closer. Above her, trees laden with snow shifted in the cold as if searching for warmer air.

To her left the ground rose up to form a small hill. At the top barbed wire marked the border. Held by wooden posts rammed into the frozen earth, it formed a line of thorns: a crown to the hill that she could not pass.

The snowmobile jolted as she struggled to keep it under control, she heard the sound of bullets passing over her shoulder.

Eve engaged the brakes and came to a stop. Pushing herself up out of the saddle she looked around. Two Russian snowmobiles bore down on her. They were supposed to be Americans she thought. We had the promise of safe passage. Or so Servitude had led her to believe. What the hell was happening?

She sat down, turned the snowmobile to the right and headed away from the border. At a hundred metres she stopped and brought herself back around to face the barbed wire.

In her mind she thought of Angerstein...

"Eyes on the job, Angerstein, you're a married man."

"... there's certain things I can't control. Especially when you walk in here looking like that."

"Is this going to work?"

"You know what? I think it just might."

Eve wished that he was here now.

Two minutes later the Russian guards found Eve tangled up in barbed wire, her snowmobile on its back like a beached turtle. Blood dripped from her arms and legs where twisted steel thrust rust into skin. Behind Eve Russian tanks approached, their red flags fluttering in the wind. Before her, in the distance, shapes appeared over the horizon on the Latvian countryside: an exodus of people carrying blankets, small children, their old following on behind.

Eve's eyelids fluttered. She opened her eyes and sighed. The world started spinning. She tried to move but the barbs dug deeper.

Shells from the tanks took to the sky and headed towards the lost, the sick, people burnt by radiation. In a few seconds they would be blown apart and burnt by their fellow man.

The border guards forced vodka down Eve's throat. Stepping back, they started emptying bullets into her soft skin.

Her eyes opened wide and the moonlight hit the back of her retinas. She followed the light within and crouched there as a small child waiting for her father. Waiting for the pain to come to an end.

CHAPTER 67

The gathering of shrouded skies.

"What's going on?" said Durram finally breaking the silence. Time started up again within the sphere as she remembered to breathe.

Pete ran for his empty space-suit and fumbled around for the Walther PPK.

"Pete," said the doppelgänger, "how lovely of you to join us. I have always wanted to do a threesome – it's so much more liberating."

"What?" said Durram. "What's happening?"

The sky grew dark. The trees cast shadows onto the ground.

Pete aimed the handgun at his doppelgänger and pulled the trigger.

Nothing.

Durram screamed.

"Oh, dear, Pete," said the impostor. "Has the little gun jammed?"

Laughter. Darkness continued to fall. Pete could hear strange sounds emanating from afar. He glanced around for something else to use as a weapon and spied Joshua's pebble lying in the snow. He snatched at it, felt its weight then cast it at his doppelgänger's forehead.

A thump and the doppelgänger fell dead to the ground.

"Arh, well that was easy," said Pete and collapsed back into the snow.

Durram rubbed her head in her hands, blinked, then sat down. Looking across she watched Pete lying exhausted and naked: his breath misting in the air. She got to her feet and walked over to him.

"Pete, what just happened?"

Pete pushed himself up, "Do you remember that you're called Durram, now?"

"Of course I'm Durram, who else would I be?"

"You're not Rebekah?"

"No."

"And I'm not Isaac?"

"No."

"Thank God for that," said Pete and lay back again, his arms outstretched in the snow.

Durram lay down beside him.

She turned and looked into Pete's eyes, her gaze locking on and holding the connection searching for the point of intersection of their two paths. Finally she spoke, "You're naked, Pete."

"As are you," said Pete staring into her dilated pupils.

The light faded. Darkness claimed the wood. Durram and Pete could hear animals in the undergrowth. A shadow passed over the ground.

"This should be it then," said Pete. "Hopefully everything will return to normal, this nightmare will end."

"I'm bloody hungry," said Durram. "Did you bring any food?"

"No, I didn't have much time, Durram."

"Chocolates? Cigarettes?"

"Durram, this is a rescue mission not a home delivery from the supermarket."

"A bunch of flowers?" said Durram smiling.

"Wait, hang on," said Pete and jumped up.

He walked over to the spacesuit, unzipped the hip pocket and pulled out the *Matthanias is Go!* apron.

"A friend gave this to me," said Pete. "You can have it if you like."

Pete passed it over the top of Durram's head and then tied the drawstrings around her back. She stood there naked apart from the apron. Pete kissed the nape of her neck and turned her around to face him.

"It suits you."

Durram punched the side of his arm. Then smiling she dropped her hand and placed it in his. "We have a lot of catching up to do."

"We do," said Pete. "Could we start with – and this is just me checking I haven't misunderstood the situation you understand – can we start with, do you want me?"

"Of course, stupid. I love you."

"You bit me the last time we met."

"Arh, that. Do we need to go over that?"

"Yes."

"Let's just take things from here," said Durram. "What happened, happened. Now is what is important."

"No, Durram. We should talk about it. I know about the abortion."

Durram looked alarmed, her body tensed.

"It's okay," said Pete. "It's okay."

Durram started to cry.

"I'm so sorry, Pete. You should leave, I'm a terrible person. I hate myself. You must hate me as well."

Pete stroked her hair, "No, Durram, I love you."

"Servitude made me do it," sobbed Durram. "It was part of going under cover, he said there was no place for children in the world I was entering."

"Servitude? That bastard."

"That's why I never contacted you, Pete. I couldn't bear to tell you."

"You should have told me."

"I couldn't."

"Did you know you were going to have the abortion when I came to see you in the hospital?"

"No, it was later that they persuaded me, after Trent shot my clone. I bit you because I had to protect you – I'd just found out that I had been state matched and married to Brittle. How could I tell you then that you were a father to children you would never see? That another man would raise them."

"Brittle's dead," said Pete. "I killed him."

"Oh my God, Pete. You what?"

"I killed him to get to Trent, Durram. I had to avenge your death."

Silence for a moment as the history of their paths filtered into their minds like water cascading over rocks to find the tranquillity of the river below. What was left unsaid at the mention of Trent was not discussed. Instead they pushed it away from them as if it were a little paper boat cast from the shore of the river.

"Did you hear that?" said Pete at a noise behind them.

"What?"

"Shh."

"What!"

"It sounds like music."

Moonlight fell and touched the creeping edge of darkness. A choir singing from far away could be heard; a violin played over the angelic voices.

The body of the doppelgänger shimmered. The snow on his body melted and formed water droplets which started to vibrate in time with the music. Eventually detaching themselves, they moving outwards from his body and formed an outline.

It shifted in fluid motions through images of leopards, lions, bears.

The ground started to bulge under him as water bubbled up from the soil. Drops lifted and floated into the air. They hung there forming a blue veil. Then a roar sounded as if coming from a great distance. The doppelgänger faded.

Pete and Durram could hear knocking. It reverberated, as thunder signalling a strike of fire from the sky.

"What was that?" said Pete.

The knocking became louder. Pete could feel the rush of hot air on his face, as if he were submerged below ground facing an oncoming train.

Muffled voices shifted through the trees ... *"It starts."*

Durram glanced around, nervous, trembling, her breathing becoming sharp as if she were running: running for her life.

The voices again ... *"Filthy rats, economic collapse, brats, bats and high rise flats. I will eat your brains out my darling."*

The knocking stopped.

It became quiet.

Pete felt for Durram's hand. Air rushed upwards in a circle around them as if being sucked out of the ground by a dust devil. The veil before them shimmered and then bowed out.

Covenant burst through. She spat out the surplus water and stood naked blinking in the light.

"Hello, children," said Covenant advancing on them.

"Who or what the hell is that?" said Durram.

"That," said Pete, "is Covenant. I think your fake boyfriend is a woman."

"I slept with a woman?"

"It would be bloody you," shouted Pete across at her. "How many times do I have to kill you? You slept with her – you bloody bastard."

"You, my darling, rather ruined my last body." She was closer now, her hands twitching by her side. "What did it feel like, beating the body of Durram to a bloody pulp on the stones of Dubrovnik?"

"What's she talking about?" said Durram.

"Never mind," said Pete.

"Arh, well, Durram. I took your form and lover boy here helped me get to sleep every night. Bless him, he's very good you know – did you teach him how to–"

"Shut it, Covenant," said Pete. "I guess you're responsible for all this?" Pete swept his hand out around the wood.

"Yes, clever boy," said Covenant. She could almost touch them. One more step. "It has a certain charm don't you think?"

Bronze-coloured leaves fluttered out of the wood like bats taking to the wing. Streaming inwards towards Covenant they covered her skin, gilding her until she shone bright like the morning sun.

"Leave us alone," said Durram.

"I enjoyed our little romps in the wood by the way, Durram," said Covenant her face before Pete. "And the river – that had a certain energy to it. I think on balance though I prefer being a woman – it's so awkward being the man, how the hell you control that thing." She wrapped her fingers around Pete's cock, "I don't know."

Pete gasped as he felt her long fingernails touch his foreskin. Durram snapped a branch from a nearby tree, leapt forward through the night air and stabbed Covenant clean through the side of her neck.

Covenant's eyes widened: became alert. She opened her mouth then composing herself pulled the branch from her neck. Drops of blood fell onto the virgin snow. Pete took a piece of flint from the floor and opened her chest in one fluid strike.

Covenant laughed, "Children. You are very naughty hurting me like that. Let me introduce myself properly. Make it all crystal clear for you, so you can decide what to do."

Pete and Durram instinctively drew back.

"I am," said Covenant speaking slowly, her words echoing around the wood. "I am the first and the last. I am the darkness that was before the light. I took Richard Trent, I ensnared Isaac Steward as Fable. I am the destroyer of worlds. I am the Leviathan. I am Mnemosyne. I am hell personified – the end of all things."

Durram looked at Pete and raised an eyebrow.

Covenant opened her mouth. A host of locusts burst out as she vomited the darkness from her soul.

"Run," said Pete. "Run like hell."

CHAPTER 68

So that they could die.

The flight through the wood disoriented Pete and Durram. Unfamiliar sounds flowed around them shrouding their reasoning: escalating emotions shaping the night into twisted creatures waiting for them to fall. Waiting to feed on flesh.

Branches clawed and snapped at their feet. The path became narrow as the wood closed in on them on either side. The primeval dread and horror of the immediacy of death driving each to lunacy as they cast themselves forward.

They stopped in a clearing and span around searching for the evil in the shapes, their minds forming faces from snatches of darkness. The wood became a blur. They ran on, not hand in hand, but in blind panic desperate to do anything to save themselves; each hoping in their hearts they would not fail the other.

She took form before them in the distance: walking slowly over the woodland floor, the sound of ravens around her, the waning moon above. Where Covenant's feet touched the ground a red glow rose up and seeped around ancient roots like a river of blood. Behind her the trees moved in to form a barrier. The sound of splintering wood, the groan of bark, the rustle of leaves, the dripping of sap.

Pete and Durram stopped, their hearts racing.

Drip. Drip. Drip.

"This way," shouted Pete.

Turning they ran back the way they'd come.

Pete sensed fingers reaching for his ankles. He could feel the hairs standing up on the back of his neck. The scent of fear in his sweat lit up his brain. He felt his skin and bones becoming rigid as if made of iron: his movement became laboured, his feet falling away, the memory of running forgotten.

When they realised that they were back where they had started, they fell exhausted to the ground. They lay aware of their own mortality ebbing away as if they were paper sails ripping and shredding before a great storm. Reaching out, their fingers touched, their hands clasped hold and they were together as one trembling.

Laughter in the wood.

She seemed to be all around them.

Durram closed her eyes and started to tremble. Pete pulled her to him and stroked her hair. Then getting to his feet he started shouting and screaming, "Come on then. Come on!" He grabbed a log and held it, his hands shaking, his heart full of her. The laughter drew nearer.

Then silence descended.

Pete saw in the corner of his eye a white dandelion seed from the great tree standing upright in the snow. Another one lay beside it and another tracing an arc ending at the spacesuit.

"Come on," he said to Durram pulling her to her feet. "We're getting out of here."

Endless choices collapsed into one swift action and leaving their fear behind in the snow as if shedding chameleon skin, they ran to the suit. Pete pulled it on and locked his helmet into place.

Holding Durram within his embrace he lifted into the air and rose up from the darkness.

CHAPTER 69

*Each one of us in our own way believes ourselves
to be immortal.*

Night passed into day and with it came a renewed sense of hope. They had flown east over mile after mile of trees, a great reforestation of the Earth and the air seemed sweeter, the sky clearer.

Pete followed the contours of the land, their shadow rising and falling with the undulations. At times he could see animals moving through the trees: elephants, monkeys, lions. As they neared the outside edge of the sphere the trees disappeared and the land dropped and opened out into a huge basin. Pete descended into a circular clearing covered in sunlight, the snow sparkling. Below hidden in winter was the invisible desert.

Durram had become still within his arms. He wondered if it wouldn't have been better if she had worn the spacesuit. He placed her down. She stirred, rubbed her eyes.

He had decided to take her back through into the world, to leave this place forever. Maybe if they could get out and return to Dubrovnik the orb would disappear.

Maybe it was her sustaining it.

What greeted him though had caused him to pause, to spend a moment considering the way forward. Before him a great wall of water rose up into the sky forming a barrier. Pete looked into it as his brain searched for patterns to form an explanation.

"It's the sea," said Durram. "The wood is devouring a great sea."

Pete had seen oceans within this world, indeed he had recognised the coastline of England, but she was right. Here there was land on their side of the sphere and a sea on the other side. The sea from his dream.

"Wow," said Durram.

"It's beautiful," said Pete. "Bloody terrifying, but beautiful."

They could hear the roar and thunder of water as the ocean emptied itself into the wall of the sphere. It appeared as if a great river a mile high and stretching far to the east and west was flowing towards them and abruptly stopping and ceasing to be.

"Are we safe?" asked Pete.

"How would I know?" said Durram. A butterfly landed on her hand. It beat its wings in the sunlight.

"Well," said Pete. "If the Pope was correct, then this is all your making."

"The Pope?"

"It's a long story. Oh my God, look."

Pete pointed towards a large sperm whale approaching in the water. For a moment it filled their view, appearing large and majestic: a great backdrop of blue to the outline of Durram and Pete. Pete imagined it was looking at them, its eye deep and mysterious. Colonies of barnacles clustered around its head. It opened its mouth revealing a row of conical teeth. Pete reached out his hand almost touching it. He could hear it clicking and buzzing trying to find a location to orient itself. Then after seventy years of being at sea it disappeared as it hit the orb.

"I suddenly feel incredibly sad," said Durram.

"I know," said Pete. "Let's go. If this is the ocean then we should be able to quickly reach an altitude where we can pass through above it. But," he stopped and looked at Durram. "We need to change driver."

Pete removed his suit and helped Durram into it.

"Have you been sweating in this? It's damp."

"Sorry," said Pete rotating the helmet into position with a click. He pulled the front zipper up over the *Matthanias is Go!* logo on the apron and knocked on top of the helmet to signal he was finished. "Okay. Now you see the control pad on your wrist? Push this button here to go up. This one controls your descent."

Durram nodded and watched as a pod of dolphins appeared in the surge of water.

"Come on," she said. "I can't take any more of this."

Pete reached out and held onto her as she started to rise, the reflection of tuna shimmering in her visor, below them the flutter of butterflies. As their feet left the ground, Pete felt a hand wrap around his ankle. Looking down he saw Covenant rise up out of the snow and ice, clumps of earth falling from her body.

She held him.

Held him tight as Durram ascended.

CHAPTER 70

What if we are not as Gods?
What if we can fall?

Durram banked to the right and started to go back to help Pete. The on-board computer aborted the manoeuvre. Failing to reconfigure to show the terraformed terrain within the sphere, it had calculated she would land in water and sink under the weight of the suit.

Battery critical. Manual Override disabled. Current location: Mediterranean Sea. Searching for nearest landmass.

She rose up instead until she could see the surface of the sea through the edge of the sphere. It was covered in small boats, trees, cast iron beds, oil drums and flotsam all being swept in her direction. Rain beat down. Great waves tipped in white froth surged forward.

She gained altitude to clear the debris. The suit pushed her towards the edge of the orb. She reached out her hand to touch it.

Warning: One percent power remaining. Please find an alternative power source.

The edge was hard: impregnable.

"Shit, now what?" she thought.

The suit traversed the boundary between the two worlds moving Durram farther away from Pete. Now and then it slammed her against the edge as if she were a ragdoll being thrown at a wall. Blood trickled over her eyes from her forehead's impact with her visor. She felt weak, tired …

Warning: One minute of power remaining.

Durram looked down. If she fell from here it would be certain death. She jabbed at the descent button but the on-board computer, stubborn to the end, refused to grant back control.

Lightning flashed over the turbulent waters. The wind picked up speed and drove the rain at her in horizontal bands so that from her perspective, in the still air of the sphere, thousands of small blue dots appeared. It was as if a code encrypted within the storm was streaming towards her.

And then without warning and without moving she was in the storm, the rain lashing her, a red glow around her as the suit wasted what little power it had left by flashing a red warning light.

She was back in the real world.

She was outside the sphere.

The roar of the water was deafening.

In that moment she thought of Pete. He was probably dead by now, his heart wrenched from his chest by the resident evil within. She had thought she could live without him, that there were other things in this world more important than love. Honour, courage, duty, purpose; she had imagined those would suffice, that with faith she would endure. But she knew now that without him all was lost. Her freedom only an illusion.

It took a moment for her to realise her suit had been penetrated by shrapnel. She moved a glove down towards her chest and saw blood pumping out from within.

The thunder moved closer. Her suit, in one last attempt to communicate with her, started playing Yazz's The Only Way Is Up: the white noise of the storm making it sound like a radio failing to lock onto a broadcast signal.

– hold on – hold on –

Looking ahead she saw the shimmering liquid hull of Matthanias rise up out of the waters, the sea falling from it as it gained height.

It had been waiting there, hiding in the water like a great white shark: following her, looking for the moment to attack. The second wave of spatial distortion mines that constantly kept step with the perimeter of the orb had been activated moments before. It had been enough to push back the outer edge thirty seconds again. It was why Durram now found herself for a brief moment on the outside of the sphere.

"Fire everything we have at her, we have about a second before the orb takes her," said Insurgent.

"We're too close," said Ira.

"Fire the damn missiles," shouted Insurgent.

Matthanias fired two missiles at Durram.

The detonation took her body and, clenching her tight within, blew Durram into a million fragments. The shock wave tore Matthanias' parallax engines clean off her side. The ship fell and sank back into the waters.

Joshua Angerstein fell to his knees and started to pray. Darkness came as Matthanias, and all the Pope had saved within her, slipped under the waves.

CHAPTER 71

My wings are clipped,
I am cast like a net.
Dash all the clocks,
light the wick.

The sound of the explosion engulfed Pete as his hands squeezed around Covenant's neck. Behind her, in the water was the reflection of Covenant as the Leviathan. Appearing as a giant sea monster she writhed and twisted towards them: her tentacles becoming flesh as they pushed through the membrane of the orb.

"What was that explosion?" said Pete. "Is Durram okay?"

"Don't stop," said Covenant to Pete, "I'm just about to come."

A tentacle from the Leviathan wrapped around Covenant's neck. Another snaked around her feet. And then with a sucking noise it was upon her and in her.

Pete released his hold.

"No," screamed Covenant at Pete. "No, here," she took his hands and placed them around her neck again. "Squeeze."

"What the hell was that thing?" said Pete.

Covenant pulled Pete into her embrace, felt his skin against hers. "God, a fight to the death," she hissed. "Just like with Aristotle, I can still remember the taste of his sweat."

Pete jabbed his fingers into her eyes, "Where is Durram?"

Covenant broke her hold and stepping back placed her hands on her hips.

"She's gone," she said running her fingers up her sides and pushing her breasts together. "Your friends have killed her." Placing her finger in her mouth she bit down and severed a fingertip. It fell to the snow in a blanket of blood. A small tentacle slithered out through the hole. "Oh, yes," she screamed. "Yes, yes, yes." She arched her back as her body went into spasm with the movement of the Leviathan inside. The tentacle slipped down her pulsating body and inserted itself into her vagina. She climaxed, then pointed, "There! Here they come now."

Within the rush of water was the ghostly outline of Matthanias. She hit the orb head on, the carbon aqua matrix of her nose disappearing. Pete could see right inside the heart of the ship as bit by bit the hull disappeared as it was drawn forward.

When the inner chambers became visible, Pete could see the horror on the crew's faces at their sudden demise. Covenant fell back into the snow and lay panting as the ship disappeared in slices as if it were a salami to a butcher's cut.

Stepping forward Pete looked into the eyes of Joshua Angerstein. He was in the toroidal lift. Behind him seawater writhed in the empty void. Seeing Pete, Joshua gasped and reached out his small hand towards him. Pete tried to take it and met instead the hard impregnable wall of the orb.

"This is too much," said Pete as Joshua disappeared. "I can't take this. You have been toying with me, Covenant, keeping me alive to see this moment, to see Durram die, to watch all that is good being undone."

Covenant smiled. The tentacle in her vagina retracted back into the hole in her severed finger and raising it to her mouth she licked it clean and then kissed it. Pete watched her fingertip grow back. Covenant rolled onto her back and opening her legs started rubbing her clitoris with her index and middle finger.

"Kill me, please," said Pete. "Kill me now."

"Sure," said Covenant, "I will ease you from this world, right after you take me. I want you inside of me now. Do that for me and I will allow you to die."

Pete slowly raised his head and met her gaze.

"No," he said. "I wasn't talking to you."

Falling to his knees, he started praying.

"Oh, please," said Covenant, closing her eyes.

CHAPTER 72

The freedom to fly.

Durram felt something wasn't quite right. For a start she was thinking and that shouldn't really be possible as she had no body having just been obliterated by a missile strike.

She also seemed to be at all places within the sphere at the same moment. She could see every tree, every animal, knew every part of the world intimately. She could see Pete kneeling before Covenant. That was wrong she thought. In fact there were a lot of things wrong. Very wrong indeed.

She imagined walking up to Covenant and found that she was there. Before her she could see Pete: his hands held behind his back by thick roots pushing out of the snow. Covenant was on her knees before him, sweat glistening on the back of her thighs, "Just warming him up for you. I can't seem to get him erect though. Be a good dear and get him nice and hard for me will you?"

Pete remained motionless. Waiting for redemption and death. Talking in distant languages under his breath he pleaded with God to take him. Every part of him streamed inwards in an implosion as he protected his heart from Covenant.

He was only able to hold on for a moment.

Then like an explosive charge detonating within he ejected up and out of his body. Behind him he carried what was precious to him – a myriad of small memories that followed the explosion as if they were attached to him by silk threads. In the multitude: the smell of grass and his leather school lunch bag, the sound of his mother's laughter and the patter of rain, the touch of Durram's kiss and the soft velvet of his dad's armchair.

In the air, he offered them all as sacrifices to his creator. Gaining height as he lost their ballast he remembered how to fly.

Below the flight of his mind, Covenant pushed her long nails into the skin on Pete's discarded body. Ten lines of blood appeared. "What's with your eyes, Durram?" she said without turning to look. "They're burning."

Durram stepped forward, "Leave him alone."

"Or you'll do what, my dear?"

Covenant started laughing.

Durram placed her hand on Covenant's back. It glowed hot and started to pass through. The tentacles from the Leviathan shot out and wrapped themselves around Durram's hand.

Durram imagined Covenant fragmenting within her mind, "You are no more."

Covenant started to shimmer. With a sudden rush of sound the fallen leaves gilding her unravelled and flew like a startled flock of birds into the air. Above they obscured the sun bringing darkness before the light burnt them away.

The Leviathan's tentacles turned to ash and fell to the floor. Covenant started to disappear, "What?" she rasped. "What's happening to me?"

Her toes disappeared, her legs, thighs, then her stomach, breasts and finally, with her eyes wide open, she vanished completely.

Pete's mind fell back to his broken husk. He opened his eyes and gasped for breath.

"Durram, you're alive!"

His wrists chafed against the roots as he struggled to break free.

"I am as God," said Durram.

"What?"

"I walk," said Durram, "in a state of bliss and wonder. Around me is the supernatural. I know all things and I am all things."

She stopped and laughing softly, span on the ground. "Pete, I cannot die. Take my arm."

The roots holding Pete recoiled back into the snow, the ten wounds on his chest healed over. He shook his head, unable to process the rapid fire of emotions thumping him as if they were defibrillators stopping his heart.

"Durram. I saw an explosion. I thought–"

"Peter, I am in ecstasy, this is amazing. All this." She swung her arms around her and pushing herself up onto the tips of her toes floated off the ground. Her hair swirled about her as if she were afloat in water. Her thighs were smoother, her stomach tighter, her breasts larger, firmer. "I couldn't see before, I didn't understand. I can control it. It's beautiful."

She giggled and took Pete's hand. Looking into his eyes she said, "I know what you fear, but you will never, never lose me again, I promise."

"Durram, I just saw a small boy die in front of my eyes. I couldn't help him, I wanted to but I couldn't."

"Shh, my darling, it's okay."

Durram took Pete and held him in her arms. She smoothed his hair and putting her hand under his chin, lifted his face and wiped away a tear. "Nothing can hurt us ever again, do you understand, Pete. We are safe."

They broke from their embrace. Butterflies flew between them.

"Well then," said Pete finally. "You're naked again, I see."

Durram laughed, "I'm afraid the suit has rather had it."

"It's gone very quiet," said Pete.

Turning they looked for the sea. It had gone, before them a vast plane filled with trees. Taking each other's hand they walked into the wood.

It seemed to Pete that Durram was at one with all around her. She appeared radiant, she glowed and smelt wonderful as if she had just bathed in a clear mountain stream. The reflection of the wood curved around the dew over her body. Light scattered from her skin as if she were a diamond formed by the Earth itself.

Every kind of tree grew around them, the sky had become a deep cobalt blue. Pete sensed he was nearing the end of his journey. He had dreamed of this, his footprints together with hers, their path as one before eternal happiness. She was his soul mate, his eternal companion; nothing would ever be the same again. The sound of a river drew them to the north.

CHAPTER 73

Her image bows out, flickers,
she still looks the same.
I reach out, touch, call out her name.
I chose you before all that would unfold,
before I became what I am now.
The smell of you the memory of summer,
the shape of you the sum of all my desires.
Together we have found the land of our hearts,
everything has become all that we can ever be.

CHAPTER 74

Tears sear the storm.

It grew dark. Stars filled the sky as if a great host had gathered. Pete and Durram held each other tight. Above them the heavens unpolluted by human light, shone radiantly.

"Shut your eyes," said Durram.

"Why?"

"I want to make everything beautiful."

Pete closed his eyes. Durram felt for his hand and threaded her fingers through his.

"Can you see me?"

"Yes," said Pete. Durram stood next to him in a field of corn.

"Come run with me and I will show you my heart."

They stood waiting with heads of wheat between them, the sound of birds in the air, the smile of connection on their faces.

Silence came as if a sleep long yearned for had finally settled upon them. A north wind played across the field and circled the crop.

In unison they broke and ran.

Swathes of wheat fell before them.

Two paths.

"Pete, let me tell you the history of the race. I love you, I have always loved you since we met. At my heart is a purity, a fairy-tale, a belief. At my heart is you."

They ran faster, ripping the ground into dust which swirled into the air.

Their pulses raced. Their hearts sang together.

Two paths become one.

Pete could feel her mingle with his senses as they came together. The past fell at their feet as they ran in the corn, the motion of movement finding serenity, a resonance. She was his nectar, the world before a broken shell. Above, the sun rose from the horizon and bathed them in light.

A thousand million suns, a thousand possibilities, all that was past all that was the future no longer mattered. And as they ran time coalesced around them holding them in a moment of bliss. Pete felt his edges blurring with hers. They were as one.

The race was won.

Durram woke Pete and passed him a leaf holding water from the lake. "Here taste it. It's sweet, it will give you energy." She laughed. "You have slept all morning, it is the middle of the afternoon."

Pete looked at her face. Her lips, thin, were smiling. Her high cheek bones were partly covered by her tumbling hair. To her right stood a snowman freshly built. Pete drank, then said, "Do you think we can get back to the real world now that she's dead?"

"You're assuming there's something to go back to."

"What do you mean?"

"I have travelled in my mind over the entire surface of this new world, Pete."

"And?"

"I can travel as far as I like to the east, west, north and south. There is no boundary, I only ever return to this point. Do you see?"

"No."

"There is no edge to the orb anymore, the earth – the old earth has gone."

"Oh, God, that is terrible," said Pete. "They are all dead? They have all gone, there is just the two of us?"

"Thanks."

"Sorry, I didn't mean it to sound like that, but billions of people have perished."

"I don't know. All I know is that this world is without end. But yes–" she stopped and felt a tear on her face for the first time since she'd been within the dome. She reached up and let it fall on her finger. She was silent for a moment, then continued, "But yes, it would seem the end came quickly for them. Hopefully they didn't suffer."

"And you can live knowing that?" said Pete.

"I can't change it, Pete. If I could, if it was down to us, then I would fall to dust to save them, but I can't."

"Are you sure she won't be back?" said Pete.

"She only had control here by keeping me in the dark as to whose world this really is. She has no power of her own."

"But if you forget yourself. If you doubt you can control all this, then there's a way back for her?"

"Well, I suppose," said Durram. "But I can hold us all together."

Pete got to his feet, "I need to pee. Nice snowman by the way."

Durram smiled.

Pete walked into the expanse of white, then stepping behind a tree relieved himself.

On his way back he bent down scooped up some snow into his palms and compacted it into a snowball. His aim was good and it thumped into Durram's side. Laughing Durram made her own snowball and returned fire. Just before it hit Pete in the face, it slowed, rotated, then came to a stop. Pete's eyes opened wide. He reached out and touched it with the end of his finger.

"Did you do that?"

Durram laughed. Small stones fell from the floating snowball as it span before him. Then it dispersed into the air around him leaving trails of blues and oranges in its wake.

"That was beautiful," said Pete.

"Thank you."

Durram turned and pointed up into the sky as more snow started to fall.

"I did that."

"You can make it snow?" said Pete standing behind her and following her gaze skyward.

"I can do anything," said Durram.

"Except work long hours," laughed Pete. "How will we know when it's after five-o'clock?"

"Is that so ingrained within you?" asked Durram.

"Of course."

"Pete, none of that matters anymore."

"You can't be serious?"

"It's a new start, Pete. We give each other time because we love each other, not because of stupid rules."

"Well," said Pete wrapping his hands around her stomach, "You're putting a lot of trust in us." He felt the soft underside of her breasts brush against his arms, kissed the side of her cheek.

Durram gasped, "Look."

In the distance a lone figure walked through the wood towards them in the cool of the day.

"I did not sense–" said Durram.

"Is it her?" interrupted Pete.

"No, it can't be," said Durram. "Quick, we must hide."

CHAPTER 75

He hears the ticking of the body clock,
it stills his mind against aftershock.
He turns for a moment and is swept away,
the battle leading him to the appointed day.

Gabriel stopped at the edge of the lake and rested for a while against one of the great boulders. He looked up; his long white linen jacket creasing at his waist. Well tailored with smart gold buttons, it had a stiff-necked collar underpinning his face.

Deep within his eyes an orange light flickered. Around his feet a blinding light shone out glowing like a furnace.

After a while he spoke.

"Why are you hiding?"

Silence.

"Come on I know you are in there."

…

"I can see the snowman – it's a bit of a giveaway."

"We are naked," said Durram.

"And you are afraid? You are as a God, Durram. You could clothe yourself if you so wished."

Pete whispered to Durram, "Could you just pull clothes out of thin air for us?"

"Of course," said Durram. "Now shh."

"But why haven't you then?"

"Shh, Pete. If you must know I like the freedom of walking around in the nude, I've kind of got used to it. And–" Durram eyed Pete up and down.

"And?" said Pete.

"Pete," said Durram. "Work it out. Look come on let's get this over with."

Pete and Durram stepped out into the clearing.

"Who are you?" said Durram. "I can't understand why I couldn't sense you."

"That is because you have to trust your imagination, Durram, not your understanding. I know you – you are the granddaughter of Abe and Keturah Steward, your sister took your grandmother's name."

"Are you the only survivor? Is everybody dead?" said Pete.

"I heard you calling me, Pete." said Gabriel. "I had rather come to my senses and hoped to avoid all this but I'm here now when it matters, before it's too late."

"Was that an answer to my question?" said Pete. "What do you mean, I called you?"

"I will tell you later if you like, it's an odd story. And yes you called me when you fell on your knees before Covenant and prayed for release." Gabriel turned to Durram. "Do you like stories?"

"Yes, I suppose."

"Good," said Gabriel. "Where would we be without stories eh?"

"Well, they're nice, but I'm sure we'd survive without them," said Durram.

"Would you now?" said Gabriel. "Well stories are everything, Durram, without them we are lost. What do you think drove the expansion of the orb? It was the story. And so this is the story of you and Pete." Gabriel indicated the world around them.

"Yes," said Durram. "This is our world."

"Well then," said Gabriel. "Let's try and keep it like this shall we?" He put his hand on Durram's shoulder. "Daughter, you are in great danger, you must lay down the power you have and give it to another."

"Why?"

Gabriel sighed, "I don't think you'll like the ending to this particular story if you don't give up your omnipotence."

"I can handle it," said Durram.

"No," said Gabriel. "You cannot. You think you have beaten the evil within this new world? Covenant was nothing, the person you should fear most, Durram, is yourself. You will be the destroyer of this land, you will take this moment with Pete and completely destroy it. You are the Behemoth."

"What the hell are you talking about?" said Pete.

"It is said," said Gabriel. "That the Behemoth and the Leviathan will interlock with one another and engage in combat in the final days."

"And?"

"Who beat the Leviathan in this world, Pete?"

"Hang on a minute," said Durram.

"In your dream, Pete," said Gabriel, "when you shed blood and sent the Behemoth and the Leviathan back into the depths it was Durram who rose from where they sank. She and the Behemoth are one and the same. You don't believe me? Here."

Gabriel placed his hand on Durram's forehead and spoke of things forming pictures in her mind. Durram's eyes flickered. Above her an aeroplane appeared, trailing behind it: twin smoke trails in the sun bleached sky.

"You are in the plane," said Gabriel. "The engines have failed."

Durram's hands started shaking.

The fasten seat belt light came on. Voices, instructions, shouting, someone praying. Durram wondered if she could remember how to get into the brace position. Should she make sure the children had fastened themselves in or connect her own belt?

She should fasten her belt.

She was about to die.

She was too young to die.

She couldn't see the kids. The fear of death rose over her, dark, brooding, hungry: she couldn't breathe. The animal instinct for survival battled with her natural desire to protect her children, the two forces clashing like titans within her skin and bone.

Before her a panoramic view of the wood opened up. She could stop this. Closing her eyes she willed it to pass.

The rows before her started disappearing.

Where was the front of the plane?

People were dying.

What the hell was going on?

She must save herself at all costs.

Then she saw her children running towards her, their arms open.

She fastened her seat belt.

Durram raised her hands to protect herself, screamed and dropped to the floor.

"Please," she murmured. "I can't trust myself. I accept him, please God take this from me."

Gabriel reached out his hand and helped her up, "Welcome my daughter."

"Oh, God," said Durram. "I thought I was about to die. I didn't help my own children. Did they make it?"

"No," said Gabriel. "But then you know that Durram. But I don't come to judge you for aborting them, I come to offer salvation."

"What the hell did you just do to her?" said Pete. "Who did you say you were again?"

"She is fine," said Gabriel. "She has laid down her divinity. And to answer your question, my name is Gabriel."

"Gabriel, as in the angel?" said Pete.

Gabriel nodded.

"Why did you have to do that to her?"

"It would have eaten away at her until she lost herself and turned to the darkness within. I know you love her and have forgiven her, Pete, but you couldn't have saved her from herself. Her pain is like a flaw in a diamond. She may appear beautiful and indestructible in her divinity but under the extreme pressure of possessing the ability to change anything, she will fracture and fall apart. And in her pain, Pete, she would have moulded you into someone you're not. Taken your essence and twisted it until she'd destroyed you."

One of the pieces of coal forming the snowman's eyes dropped to the floor.

"Do not judge her, Pete, we all have a great darkness within."

"What about me?" said Pete.

"You have believed for a very long time, Pete. How do you think you entered into this world? You hide it well sometimes though, I grant you. Perhaps in the future you could be a little more confident and trust in God more than you trust in your own understanding? Use a bit more of that imagination you have – make up some stories again – don't squander your gift.

"So wonderful, let's make this official then shall we? Pete, I give you Durram. Durram, I give you Pete."

"Sorry, have you just married us?"

"No, Pete, she is your reward and you are hers."

Pete and Durram glanced at each other.

"It's a happily ever after thing," said Gabriel. "There is no marriage here, only fairy tale endings. Kiss her then, Pete."

Pete took Durram and drawing her to him, kissed her lips and threaded his fingers into hers.

"Oh, and Pete," said Gabriel. "You are going to have to take special care of her for a while."

"A while?"

"Yes, about nine months."

"I'm pregnant?" asked Durram.

"Congratulations," said Gabriel.

Inside Durram a hollow formed. The heat of the sun pulled tears leaving salt lining her stomach. It cracked and bled causing pain.

"You are pregnant with your children and you will be fine, don't worry," said Gabriel. "Twins in fact you are going to have your hands full."

"Thank you," said Pete.

Durram squeezed his hand.

"Now here," said Gabriel. "Another gift."

Gabriel handed him Durram's Generation Game trading cards. "Something to pass away the evenings with Durram."

Gabriel started to walk back amongst the trees, then stopping he added, "Oh by the way I forgot to say. Your babies will have someone to play with once they're old enough. I saved this little chap." Gabriel pushed him forward. "Once I'd pulled myself together, I plucked him from the water just in the nick of time. You'll like him, he certainly brought me to my senses – I think you've already met him, Pete? Kid by the name of Joshua Angerstein. He tells some cracking stories, taught by the very best I understand. Say hello, Joshua."

"Hello," said Joshua Angerstein.

EPILOGUE

The bark is a skin weathered by sun, wind, rain, snow. A history of time marked out as the tree orbits the sun. Rings growing ever outward around its pith like the planetary halo of a large planet. Its heartwood stronger than iron, rising water in its sapwood bringing life from soil to stars.

Durram

Durram held the twins to her breasts. They nuzzled there and finding a nipple each, drank from their mother. She smiled and when they were full she took them to the crystal river. There she held them in her embrace and watched her son, Joshua, skim his father's stone across the waters. And she gave thanks to God for her family. A family where death would be forever absent. A life that would endure, bring fruit, bring happiness.

A canopy of mottled greens encircle the tree, a wood without end: the white froth of clouds dancing upon them. Rivers below flowing like liquid gold in the dappled sunlight. Questions thrown as seeds into the wind looking for soil to take root, to explain, to answer: why?

Pete

Pete watched as one of the dandelion seeds pushed up. Higher and higher it rose, and thicker and thicker it became, until the huge trunk of The Dandelion Tree soared up before him. Shade fell as branches grew. Emerald leaves sprouted, filling the air with a sweet aroma. Fruit swelled up and tugged down on slender branches. Pete smiled and picked up the wood he had harvested earlier. Today would be the day he started work on their family treehouse. All he needed now was a monkey and his life

244

would be complete. Durram would be his Jane and he her Tarzan.

In the air around the tree are the sounds of stories diffused into heart beats, rhythms left over from words. The folly of man looking for understanding held by roots in ancient earth. What endures is woven into the landscape: beauty, love, hope, connection.

Sweeping over the topography brings branches, bluebells, grasses, a sweet aroma from broad evergreen leaves. Within the tree are Pete and Durram. The colours and light of the wood pass over them like sheets of billowing russet. Skin, bone, bark and fern become one. They watch a great waterfall, their eyelids flickering to slow their perception of time – water droplets become gems of blue jasper suspended in the air.

They climb, finding connection with their fingers in the wooden skin until they sit looking out over the wood, their hair blowing in the wind, their bodies tinged in blue. They scatter colours from the sky as the sunlight hits their skin as if their beads of sweat are dustings of sapphires and amethyst.

Gabriel

Gabriel watched as the Spirit hovered over the waters and wondered on the power of the imagination to connect with the divine. Getting up he walked over the lake. Shimmering fish appearing under his feet in golds and blues. When he reached the middle, he fell to his knees and bowed his head; then turning and stretching out his arms, he floated on his back feeling the warmth of the sun on his face.

Man, fire, machines, hate, violence; all pound at the door wanting to be let in. Doctrinal keys fail in locks responding only to the voices of those woven into narratives: the story is everything. And everything has become the story. Take it as a bird in your hand and let it fly free.

Forever and ever.

There is no end.

Elsewhen Press
a small independent publisher specialising in Speculative Fiction

Visit the Elsewhen Press website at elsewhen.co.uk for the latest information on all of our titles, authors and events; to read our blog; find out where to buy our books and ebooks; or to place an order.

Elsewhen Press

a small independent publisher specialising in Speculative Fiction

THE ASCENT OF
ISAAC STEWARD
MIKE FRENCH

THE DANDELION TRILOGY
BOOK 1

Literary surrealism at its most profound, *The Ascent of Isaac Steward* follows one man's journey into his own mind as he struggles to come to terms with the trauma that has reshaped his life.

A year on from the car crash in which his wife Rebekah and son Esau were killed and his other son Jacob left in a coma, Isaac Steward has suppressed every memory of that fateful day. Yet fate seems determined to make him remember, driving Isaac deeper and deeper into himself. Slowly, dysfunction builds on delusion, as childhood memories compete with a persona he has fabricated to regress to an earlier, happier time. Violence, death and destruction result as Isaac gradually loses his grip on reality. His half-brother Ishmael tells him that he must return to the wood at his childhood home, to a tree he called The Dandelion Tree, if he is ever to be reunited with Rebekah. But as he descends further, he starts to question his own existence.

ISBN: 9781908168351 (epub, kindle)
ISBN: 9781908168252 (224pp paperback)

Visit bit.ly/IsaacSteward

Elsewhen Press

a small independent publisher specialising in Speculative Fiction

BLUE FRIDAY
MIKE FRENCH

THE DANDELION TRILOGY
BOOK 2

In the Britain of 2034 overtime for married couples is banned, there is enforced viewing of family television (much of it repeats of old shows from the sixties and seventies), monitored family meal-times and a coming of age where twenty-five year-olds are automatically assigned a spouse by the state computer if they have failed to marry. Only the Overtime Underground network resists.

Dystopian science fiction, *Blue Friday* tells of a future where many live in fear of the Family Protection Agency, a special police division enforcing the strict legislation that has been introduced to protect the family unit. Combining dark humour with a vision of the future that inverts the classic dystopian nightmare, this latest novel from Mike French follows in the tradition of great Speculative Fiction satirists such as Jonathan Swift. Thoughtful, while at the same time prompting a wry smile in the reader, it reverses the usual perception of a future regime driven by productivity and industrial output at the expense of family, demonstrating that the converse may be no better.

ISBN: 9781908168177 (epub, kindle)
ISBN: 9781908168078 (192pp paperback)

Visit bit.ly/Blue_Friday

Elsewhen Press

a small independent publisher specialising in Speculative Fiction

The Lost Men
An Allegory
David Colón

In a world where the human population has been decimated, self-reliance is the order of the day. Of necessity, the few remaining people must adapt residual technology as far as possible, with knowledge gleaned from books that were rescued and have been treasured for generations. After a childhood of such training, each person is abandoned by their parents when they reach adulthood, to pursue an essentially solitary existence. For most, the only human contact is their counsel, a mentor who guides them to find 'the one', their life mate as decreed by Fate. Lack of society brings with it a lack of taboo, ensuring that the Fate envisioned by a counsel is enacted unquestioningly. The only threats to this stable, if sparse, existence are the 'lost men', mindless murderers who are also self-sufficient but with no regard for the well-being of others, living outside the confines of counsel and Fate.

Is Fate a real force, or is it totally imagined, an arbitrary convention, a product of mankind's self-destructive tendency? In this allegorical tale, David Colón uses an alternate near-future to explore the boundaries of the human condition and the extent to which we are prepared to surrender our capacity for decisions and self-determination in the face of a very personally directed and apparently benevolent, authoritarianism. Is it our responsibility to rebuke inherited 'wisdom' for the sake of envisioning and manifesting our own will?

David Colón is an Assistant Professor of English at TCU in Fort Worth, Texas, USA. Born and raised in Brooklyn, New York, he received his Ph.D. in English from Stanford University and was a Chancellor's Postdoctoral Fellow in English at the University of California, Berkeley. His writing has appeared in numerous journals, including *Cultural Critique, Studies in American Culture, DIAGRAM, How2*, and *MELUS*. *The Lost Men* is his first book.

ISBN: 9781908168146 (epub, kindle)
ISBN: 9781908168047 (192pp paperback)

Visit lost-men.com

Elsewhen Press

a small independent publisher specialising in Speculative Fiction

LiGa™

Sanem Ozdural

Welcome.

You are hereby invited to compete in a tournament of LifeGame™ Bridge ("LiGa™ Bridge"). LiGa™ Bridge is a tournament of duplicate individual bridge in which eight players gamble with, and for, a portion of their lives.

Yes, it is possible to gamble with life! We have the technology.

You will be gambling with a portion of your remaining life to win a portion of the other players' lives. Each player will wager one third of his/her remaining life per game, as measured by Life Points, to win one quarter of the total Life Points deposited by the losing four players. The losers' remaining lives will be shortened by one third.

The tournament ends when one – or more – of the players reaches 100 Life Points, the point at which the age-related degeneration of the human body ceases completely, irreversibly, and indefinitely. This does not mean you cannot be killed, only that you will not age.

If you wish to enter the tournament you must submit a non-refundable entrance fee of $10,000,000.00.

Xavier Redd (Imm.)

Have YOU had your invitation yet?

Literary science fiction, LiGa™ tells of a game in which the players are, literally, gambling with their lives. Sanem Ozdural's debut novel is set in a near-future where a secretive organisation has developed technology to transfer the regenerative power of a body's cells from one person to another, conferring extended or even indefinite life expectancy. As a means of controlling who benefits from the technology, access is obtained by winning a tournament of chess or bridge to which only a select few are invited. At its core, the game is a test of a person's integrity, ability and resilience.

The fantastic nature of the game's technology is made credible by the familiarity of the contemporary setting, giving the story a definite slipstream feel. Sanem's novel provides a fascinating insight into the motivation both of those characters who win and thus have the possibility of virtual immortality and of those who will effectively lose some of their life expectancy.

ISBN: 9781908168160 (epub, kindle)
ISBN: 9781908168061 (400pp paperback)

Visit http://bit.ly/BookLiGa

Elsewhen Press
a small independent publisher specialising in Speculative Fiction

ENTANGLEMENT
DOUGLAS THOMPSON

FINALLY, TRAVEL TO THE STARS IS HERE

In 2180, travel to neighbouring star systems has been mastered thanks to quantum teleportation using the 'entanglement' of sub-atomic matter; astronauts on earth can be duplicated on a remote world once the dupliport chamber has arrived there. In this way a variety of worlds can be explored, but what humanity discovers is both surprising and disturbing, enlightening and shocking. Each alternative to mankind that the astronauts find, sheds light on human shortcomings and potential while offering fresh perspectives of life on Earth. Meanwhile, at home, the lives of the astronauts and those in charge of the missions will never be the same again.

Best described as philosophical science fiction, *Entanglement* explores our assumptions about such constants as death, birth, sex and conflict, as the characters in the story explore distant worlds and the intelligent life that lives there. It is simultaneously a novel and a series of short stories: multiple worlds, each explored in a separate chapter, a separate story; every one another step on mankind's journey outwards to the stars and inwards to our own psyche. Yet the whole is much greater than the sum of the parts; the synergy of the episodes results in an overarching story arc that ultimately tells us more about ourselves than about the rest of the universe.

Douglas Thompson's short stories have appeared in a wide range of magazines and anthologies. He won the Grolsch/Herald Question of Style Award in 1989 and second prize in the Neil Gunn Writing Competition in 2007. His first book, *Ultrameta*, published in 2009, was nominated for the Edge Hill Prize, and shortlisted for the BFS Best Newcomer Award. *Entanglement* is his fifth novel.

ISBN: 9781908168153 (epub, kindle)
ISBN: 9781908168054 (336pp paperback)

Visit bit.ly/EntanglementBook

Elsewhen Press

a small independent publisher specialising in Speculative Fiction

THE FIRST BOOK IN THE
INVERSE SHADOWS UNIVERSE

SUFFICIENTLY
ADVANCED
TECHNOLOGY
CHRISTOPHER NUTTALL

For the post-singularity Confederation, manipulating the quantum foam – the ability to alter the base code of the universe itself and achieve transcendence – is the holy grail of science. But it seems an impossible dream until their scouts encounter Darius, a lost colony world whose inhabitants have apparently discarded the technology that brought them to the planet in order to adopt a virtually feudal culture. On Darius, the ruling elite exhibits abilities that defy the accepted laws of physics. They can manipulate the quantum foam!

Desperate to understand what is happening on Darius, the Confederation dispatches a stealth team to infiltrate the planet's society and discover the truth behind their strange abilities. But they will soon realise that the people on Darius are not all the simple folk that they seem – and they are sitting on a secret that threatens the entire universe ...

Christopher Nuttall has been planning sci-fi books since he learned to read. Born and raised in Edinburgh, Chris created an alternate history website and eventually graduated to writing full-sized novels. Studying history independently allowed him to develop worlds that hung together and provided a base for storytelling. After graduating from university, Chris started writing full-time. As an indie author he has self-published a number of novels, but this is his fourth fantasy to be published by Elsewhen Press. *Sufficiently Advanced Technology* is his fourth novel to be published by Elsewhen Press, and the first in the Inverse Shadows universe. Chris is currently living in Borneo with his wife, muse, and critic Aisha.

ISBN: 9781908168344 (epub, kindle)
ISBN: 9781908168245 (336pp, paperback)

Visit bit.ly/SAT-Nuttall

Elsewhen Press

a small independent publisher specialising in Speculative Fiction

[RE]AWAKENINGS

AN ANTHOLOGY OF NEW SPECULATIVE FICTION

• ALISON BUCK • NEIL FAARID • GINGERLILY •

• ROBIN MORAN • PR POPE • ALEXANDER SKYE •

• PETER WOLFE •

[Re]Awakenings are the starting points for life-changing experiences; a new plane of existence, an alternate reality or cyber-reality. This genre-spanning anthology of new speculative fiction explores that theme with a spectrum of tales, from science fiction to fantasy to paranormal; in styles from clinically serious to joyfully silly. As you read through them all, and you must read all of them, you will discover along the way that stereo-typical distinctions between the genres within speculative fiction are often arbitrary and unhelpful. You will be taken on an emotional journey through a galaxy of sparkling fiction; you will laugh, you will cry; you will consider timeless truths and contemplate eternal questions.

All of life is within these pages, from birth to death (and in some cases beyond). In all of these stories, most of them specifically written for this anthology, the short story format has been used to great effect. If you haven't already heard of some of these authors, you soon will as they are undoubtedly destined to become future stars in the speculative fiction firmament. Remember, you read them here first!

[Re]Awakenings is a collection of short stories from exciting new voices in UK speculative fiction, compiled by guest editor PR Pope. It contains the following stories: Alison Buck: *Dreamers; Intervention; Mirror mirror; Podcast.* Neil Faarid: *The Adventures of Kit Brennan: Kidnapped!* Gingerlily: *The Dragon and the Rose.* Robin Moran: *The Merry Maiden Wails.* PR Pope: *Afterlife; Courtesy Bodies; On the Game.* Alexander Skye: *BlueWinter; Dreaming Mars; Exploring the Heavens; Worth it.* Peter Wolfe: *If you go into the woods today…*

ISBN: 9781908168108 (epub, kindle)
ISBN: 9781908168009 (288pp paperback)

Visit bit.ly/ReAwakenings

Elsewhen Press

a small independent publisher specialising in Speculative Fiction

A Life Less Ordinary
Christopher Nuttall

There is magic in the world, hiding in plain sight. If you search for it, you will find it, or it will find you. Welcome to the magical world.

Having lived all her life in Edinburgh, the last thing 25-year old Dizzy expected was to see a man with a real (if tiny) dragon on his shoulder. Following him, she discovered that she had stumbled from her mundane world into a parallel magical world, an alternate reality where dragons flew through the sky and the Great Powers watched over the world. Convinced that she had nothing to lose, she became apprenticed to the man with the dragon. He turned out to be one of the most powerful magicians in all of reality.

But powerful dark forces had their eye on this young and inexperienced magician, intending to use her for the ultimate act of evil – the apocalyptic destruction of all reality. If Dizzy does not realise what is happening to her and the worlds around her, she won't be able to stop their plan. A plan that will ravage both the magical and mundane worlds, consuming everything and everyone in fire.

Christopher Nuttall has been planning sci-fi books since he learned to read. Born and raised in Edinburgh, Chris created an alternate history website and eventually graduated to writing full-sized novels. Studying history independently allowed him to develop worlds that hung together and provided a base for storytelling. After graduating from university, Chris started writing full-time. As an indie author, he has self-published a number of novels. *A Life Less Ordinary* is his third fantasy novel to be published by Elsewhen Press. Chris is currently living in Borneo with his wife, muse, and critic Aisha.

ISBN: 9781908168337 (epub, kindle)
ISBN: 9781908168238 (336pp, paperback)

Visit bit.ly/ALLO-Nuttall

About the Author

Mike French is the owner and senior editor of the prestigious literary magazine, *The View From Here* which has been called many fine things since it started in 2007 including, "Attractive, informative, sparkling and useful" by the late Iain M. Banks and for having a "great passion and drive" by Booker shortlisted Tom McCarthy. Mike's debut novel, *The Ascent of Isaac Steward*, the first book of the Dandelion Trilogy, was published in 2011 and nominated for a Galaxy National Book Award which, presumably due to an unfortunate clerical error, was awarded to Dawn French. The second book in the trilogy, the satirical *Blue Friday*, was published in 2012. *Convergence* is the final part of the trilogy.

Born in Cornwall in 1967, Mike spent his childhood flipping between England and Scotland with a few years in between in Singapore. Splitting his time between his own writing, editing the magazine, running author workshops and working with atp media in Luton, Mike is married with three children and a growing number of pets. He currently lives in Luton in the UK and when not working watches Formula 1, eats Ben & Jerry's Phish Food and listens to Noah and the Whale.